TEMPORARY
TIMES,
TEMPORARY
PLACES

A CHARLOTTE ZOLOTOW BOOK

Also by Barbara Robinson

THE BEST CHRISTMAS PAGEANT EVER

TEMPORARY TIMES, TEMPORARY PLACES

BARBARA ROBINSON

1 8  1 7

———— HARPER & ROW, PUBLISHERS ————

Cambridge, Philadelphia, San Francisco, London, Mexico City, São Paulo, Sydney

———— NEW YORK ————

Temporary Times, Temporary Places
Copyright © 1982 by Barbara Robinson
All rights reserved. No part of this book may be
used or reproduced in any manner whatsoever without
written permission except in the case of brief quotations
embodied in critical articles and reviews. Printed in
the United States of America. For information address
Harper & Row, Publishers, Inc., 10 East 53rd Street,
New York, N.Y. 10022. Published simultaneously in
Canada by Fitzhenry & Whiteside Limited, Toronto.

Library of Congress Cataloging in Publication Data
Robinson, Barbara.
  Temporary times, temporary places.

  Summary: The joy and pain of first love form a bond
between a teenage girl and her aunt when they discover
they share the same feelings about their individual
love affairs.
  [1. Aunts—Fiction] I. Title.
PZ7.R5628Te 1982   [Fic]   81-47732
ISBN 0-06-025039-9   AACR2
ISBN 0-06-025042-9 (lib. bdg.)

This book is for Margie with love

TEMPORARY TIMES, TEMPORARY PLACES

Chapter One 🌿

I didn't know, when school ended in June, that there was going to be anything extraordinary about that vacation. In fact, it began on a low note, when my Aunt May arrived at our house to stay for a while and—because her heart was broken and her life a shambles—took over my room.

"Poor May," everyone said, but my mother also sighed at me and said, "Poor you," and helped me move my clothes and treasures into my grandmother's room where everything was old and out of date, by Grandma's own choice—a much-mended afghan, a dish of chalky peppermints on the night table, a series of faded Wallace Nutting prints, marching in dreary precision along the wall. It was a little old lady's room, and I was fifteen years old. But there was no help for it—after all, I had to sleep someplace and the only place was with Grandma.

When I was very small I wouldn't have minded this, because I always used to look forward to Aunt May's overwhelming arrivals—she introduced into my tranquil existence much color and drama . . . not to mention a steady stream of wholly inappropriate gifts. Aunt May always bought me things which she would like to have herself, regardless of her age or mine—jewelry, perfume, elaborate pocketbooks—so of course I loved them all, up to and beyond the moment when my mother firmly took them from me and put them away, for when I was older, or bigger, or had "any reason to carry a beaded evening bag!"

But inevitably we had grown . . . not so much apart, as separate. I had other interests, other friends, other sources of color and drama (however muted) in my life. And Aunt May had troubles, one upon the other.

Her present broken heart and shambled life were nothing new. She had been married twice and twice divorced and was done in now because she couldn't get married again. The man was already married and had children, and though he loved Aunt May—or so she said he told her—he could not abandon his family. Aunt May didn't want him to do that anyway. It was hard to figure out just what she *did* want.

And so she came home . . . but by no means like

some wounded animal seeking shelter. Aunt May was a stormy woman, and she arrived, appropriately enough, in a barrage of summer thunder and lightning that sent our dog Pansy to huddle, quivering, under the dining-room table.

We watched from the front window as Aunt May got out of a taxicab and then stood there with the elements crashing all around her, talking to the driver. We could almost hear what she was saying, over the thunder, for her voice (like everything else about her) was uninhibited. My grandmother jittered back and forth, wringing her hands.

"Oh, why won't she come on in?" Grandma said—not because of getting wet but because of maybe being struck by lightning, which was one of Grandma's basic fears. She especially worried about this in connection with Aunt May, for Aunt May seemed like an ideal subject to be struck by lightning.

But she escaped this time, dismissed the taxicab, and rampaged into the house, smelling of Shalimar perfume and Hind's Honey and Almond Lotion. Aunt May was said to be beautiful, and though my notions of beauty ran more to the likes of Bootsie Duvendeck (head cheerleader, bundle of energy, full of freckles and fun), I could see how Aunt May got her reputation. Tall, red-haired, flamboyant in dress and manner, it was hard to overlook her, and even now, soaking wet, she was an impressive figure. She dropped her suitcases by the door, flung her coat in

one direction and her hat in another, kissed us all—
big noisy smacks—but reserved her real welcome for
Pansy, who wriggled out from under the table, daring
even the terrors of the storm to greet Aunt May.

Then she plumped herself down on the sofa, rum-
maged through her squashy pocketbook for a cigarette, and took a long, nose-pinching drag, sending
forth clouds of smoke. Characteristically, Aunt May
always seemed to get more smoke out of her cigarettes
than anybody else.

You would have said, had you been there, that this
was no heartbroken woman. That was certainly my
thought.

Eventually the three of them—Mother, Grandma,
and Aunt May—went out to the kitchen and sat
around the table, drinking coffee, while Aunt May
told all. Naturally, I wasn't invited, but it didn't make
any difference . . . what Aunt May had to say she
said at the top of her lungs, so I heard the whole
story, which was, as I've already stated, one of hopeless love on the part of all concerned. I listened, too,
to every word, for I was involved in a similar predica-
ment.

I was not, to be sure, in love with any married
man, but I might as well have been. I was in love
with Eddie Walsh, who could take his pick of any
girl in town, and consequently couldn't see me for
dust. Indeed, so hopeless and helpless was this passion
that I willingly shared it with my best friend Marilyn

Ruggles, who was also in love with Eddie Walsh.

We didn't have anyone else to *be* in love with, Marilyn and I, because we weren't among those happy few who found it easy to be with boys, to talk to boys, to think of boys as just part of the general population. Whenever we were around boys we stuck together like Siamese twins, so we'd be sure to have someone to talk to, and our only dates so far had been the "Let's all go to the movies" variety, and never seemed to include the boys you would choose to go to the movies with.

We certainly weren't satisfied with this situation, but we weren't frantic yet, either . . . except when it came to Eddie Walsh. There was no jealousy involved here—he was so far out of reach for both of us—and we sat around for hours dreaming up romantic adventures with Eddie, planning complicated accidental meetings, studying the daily horoscopes (his and ours) in the hope that astrological destiny would work where nothing else did.

When we weren't together we were on the phone, talking about Eddie; when we went to the movies we spent all our time looking around to see if Eddie was there and who he was with . . . and every Sunday evening we got dressed to the teeth and sallied off to the Methodist Youth Fellowship meeting because that was where Eddie went every Sunday evening. I was a Presbyterian and Marilyn was a Baptist, but that was beside the point. We happily put our movie money into the Methodist plate, learned the Methodist hymns (they were better anyway), and had every hopeful expectation of attending the Methodist youth retreat at Lake Clement, later that summer.

Because of all this I should perhaps have been more sympathetic toward Aunt May's situation, but in my view Aunt May was old—thirty-nine or forty, I guess, at that time—and while I could imagine her loving someone in a companionable sort of way, I couldn't imagine her being in love as I was—all pins and needles and hope and despair.

"Oh, May, May," I heard my mother say, "why do you let yourself be hurt this way? You must have known he was married."

No, she hadn't at first, and then later it hadn't seemed important.

"Important to whom?" Grandma asked. "Him? You? His wife . . . his children?"

My interest in the kitchen conversation evaporated, for now it was clearly going to turn on morals: Aunt May's, the man's, my grandmother's . . . and I went upstairs to my room and closed the door.

Closed door or not, it was no longer my room. It already smelled of Shalimar, and Aunt May had emptied her train case on the dresser top in a jumble of lipsticks and nail polish and candy mints and matchbooks and a lot of big bright chunky jewelry which she loved. It occurred to me that Aunt May was a person out of her proper time. She would have made a great courtesan in the days before the French Revolution when (as far as I could tell from our history lessons) nobody's heart ever got broken.

The telephone rang, and it was Marilyn, and we talked for twenty-five minutes. The gist of her news was that, without plan or purpose, she had run smack into Eddie Walsh at the library. That was really all she had to say, but of course I had to hear every last detail: what he was wearing, where he was sitting, what he was doing, what he said, what she said (nothing, as it turned out—too thunderstruck by the encounter) . . . on and on and on, until my mother came out of the kitchen, looking troubled and unhappy. She was not, however, too troubled and unhappy to tell me to get off the phone and go along to bed.

I did, and had the bed to myself for a while . . . to lie there and dream about Eddie; to picture him (as described by Marilyn) sitting at the long library table, wearing the blue sweater that matched his eyes; to conjure up a whole slick, snazzy conversation in case I ever had a stroke of luck like Marilyn's.

But then, all too soon, I heard Mother and Grandma talking as they came upstairs to bed; heard the front door slam behind Aunt May, off to take Pansy around the block. Besides adoring all the wrong men, Aunt May adored all animals, and I thought how happy Pansy must be to have her here. The rest of us paid a price for Aunt May's presence: I lost my room,

Mother and Grandma their peace of mind, my father—out of town and all unknowing—had lost his privacy . . . but Pansy would live high on the hog and be a petted darling for as long as Aunt May was with us.

Grandma tiptoed into the room, still muttering to herself and sighing long heavy sighs as she shed her clothes and put on her nightgown, all this in the dark as usual—whether for reasons of economy or modesty, I had never figured out. Then she leaned over me, whispered "Janet?" . . . and when I didn't answer, tucked the sheet around my shoulders as if I were five or six years old, and climbed into bed.

The next day my father returned from his business trip, bringing with him a blistering heat wave which proved to be a blessing in disguise. I nearly suffocated in Grandma's airless little room, and she was probably just as uncomfortable with me thrashing around all night, so Mother let me get out the rollaway cot and set it up by the windows in the upstairs hall. It was a nuisance as long as people were getting ready for bed and going in and out of the bathroom, but once the bedroom doors were closed and everyone asleep, it was as if I had the whole house to myself, with its muffled tickings and creakings and, outside my windows, the sound of crickets, the two late-night trains to Cincinnati, and the brush of branches against the side of the house.

I never moved back to my grandmother's bed, much

to everyone's dismay. I couldn't possibly get a good night's sleep on the cot, they said; and I was sure to catch summer pneumonia from the draft up the stairs. Mainly, though, I think this sleeping arrangement was just too loose and casual for everyone's comfort.

"Like gypsies," Grandma said, with a little sniff and (as far as I knew) no personal knowledge at all of gypsies; and my mother said it didn't seem right for a member of the family to be sleeping in a hallway when there were beds and bedrooms available. But my father said for everyone to let me alone, and I would probably get tired of it soon enough.

After that there was less grumbling, and when the weather cooled off a little Mother put a summer blanket at the foot of the cot and added two or three fancy pillows—to make the whole thing look less like a bed, I guess, and more like a decorative feature of the upstairs hall.

This unorthodox setup was especially suited to the temper of that summer's times, for it was the last of my footloose summers. By the time another vacation rolled around I would be sixteen, and like everyone else who was sixteen, I would get a summer job— an already-promised one, in fact, behind the counter at Slattery's Drugstore. Marilyn was going to work part-time in her Uncle Fred's insurance agency.

Meanwhile, though, there was one bright-blue day after another which I cheerfully frittered away as if such days came from an inexhaustible bottle labeled

"SUMMER." Marilyn and I played tennis and went swimming and washed our hair and tried to find the dirty books in the library . . . and, finding *Gone With the Wind*, thought we had one. And, as often as was reasonable, we visited the A&P, where Eddie Walsh worked.

From time to time in our travels we ran across Aunt May, coming out of the movies or waiting for a bus or buying Shalimar perfume at the cosmetics counter where we went to squirt ourselves with the free samples. Sometimes she saw us, sometimes not—on the whole I liked it better when she didn't, because such chance meetings with your grown-ups could cut you down. Feeling loose and sassy and on your own, you might meet your mother on the street and right away she would want to know where you were going and what you were doing and why in the world you wore *that* blouse . . . and it might take as long as an hour for you to feel again the way you felt before.

In all fairness, Aunt May never had quite this dampening an effect, probably because she was so clearly a different breed of cat. Mother, for instance, never went to the movies in the afternoon, and when she went downtown shopping, she went shopping *for* something—cotton underwear, dish towels, a new rubber mat for the bathtub so Grandma wouldn't fall and break her hip.

Of course, in time—about three weeks—we ran out of things to do, or rather, the things we had to do ran out of charm, except for hanging around the A&P, and we couldn't spend twenty-four hours a day doing that.

We were bored with ourselves and with each other and bored especially with the very thing we had looked forward to—lazy ease.

"We need to do something constructive," Marilyn said—and the constructive thing we thought up to do made my mother laugh.

"Plan a party!" she said. "Why not clean out the basement, that's very constructive. . . . Oh, I guess you can go ahead and have a party. Why not? . . . Does it have to be an overnight?"

We said it did.

"Can we ask my cousin?" Marilyn said. "My cousin, Peggy Watkins . . . they're coming to visit us."

Mother laughed again. "Why, Peggy Watkins must be twenty, twenty-one years old by now! What makes you think she'd want to go to an overnight party with all you girls?"

"Well, at least we ought to ask her," I said.

"Well . . . maybe so. But pick a night when your father will be away. It bothers him to have people sleeping all over the living room—he thinks they ought to be sleeping in beds. And I wouldn't count on Peggy Watkins."

But to Mother's surprise (and a little to mine) Peggy came, and added a whole new glamorous dimension to the evening because she turned out to be newly engaged. I don't know why she chose to spend that night with six giggly girls unless she had run out of people to show her engagement ring to, but if that was the reason, she made a good choice, because we were a perfect audience.

It was the least boisterous overnight party I had ever been to: we all just sat around and listened to Peggy and studied her engagement ring and tried it on—had it been her wedding ring, she told us, we wouldn't be able to try it on because she planned never to take her wedding ring off but to be buried with it; and we all filed that romantic intention away for future reference.

I thought, with some embarrassment, of my mother, who was forever taking her wedding ring off—when she made bread or mixed up turkey stuffing or scrubbed down the kitchen. Even worse, she didn't pin it to her dress or put it carefully away in her jewel box; she simply hung it on the broom nail with the whisk broom and the dustpan where, she said, she would know where it was.

We heard about Peggy's wedding plans (dress, flowers, music); her honeymoon (a secret); shower gifts she had received and other gifts she hoped to receive . . . chiefly a pressure cooker, without which, she said, she would never be able to get a meal on the table. She considered it the indispensable kitchen tool and we all agreed, although I, for one, was scared pea green by our pressure cooker, which blew up almost every time Grandma tried to use it.

The only sound in the living room, aside from the crunch of potato chips and the record player on low, was Peggy's voice, and so I was honestly surprised when Aunt May called down from the top of the stairs for us to shut up and let other people get some sleep. This happened at every overnight party I ever went to, but usually with just cause. This time I couldn't see what Aunt May was yelling about, and I marched upstairs to say so.

"What's the matter?" I said. "We weren't making any noise at all. Peggy was just telling us . . ."

I don't think Aunt May heard a word I said. "Don't you have any consideration?" she demanded, in her voice like a trumpet. "How do you think anyone can sleep with you down there, laughing and talking and carrying on? I don't know what your mother's thinking of. . . . I wouldn't have a house full of silly girls. . . ." She stormed on and on, hardly pausing for breath; certainly she didn't pause to hear what I had to say, which was the same thing over and over—"I told you we weren't making any noise!"

There we stood, yelling at each other—I could hear Mother scrambling out of bed—and then Aunt May hauled off and slapped me.

I had been slapped before so I didn't cave in from shock, but I had rarely been slapped with such force and fury. Mother came hurrying out of her bedroom, her eyes wide with alarm, saying, "Hush . . .

hush . . . what in the world is the matter? For heaven's sake, May, you look like a wild woman!"

"She slapped me in the face," I said. I could feel the exact mark of her hand, as if all five fingers were welted there on my cheek.

"Yes . . . Well . . ." Mother took me by the shoulders and turned me toward the bathroom. "You go bathe your face and May, you come and sleep in my bed. It'll be quieter for you. . . ."

But Aunt May flung Mother's arm aside and flounced back into her room, slamming the door behind her.

"It isn't fair," I said. "We weren't making any noise at all."

The trouble for Mother, I suppose, was that she knew the truth of that. She had lived through enough overnight parties to realize that this one was unique in terms of peacefulness. On the other hand, she knew what had really caused the uproar—Peggy's detailed account of young love coming to its logical conclusions . . . at a time when Aunt May's love was neither young nor coming to any conclusion at all. "Whatever possessed that Peggy Watkins to come?" I heard Mother mutter, and then she put her arm around my shoulders. "You just go on back and all of you lie down and try to get some sleep."

"But we weren't making any noise!" Being in the right for once, I was like a dog with a bone.

"Yes, I know . . . but remember your Aunt May

isn't used to having young people around." She paused a moment. "And she's restless."

Restless . . . I guess. I could hear her for hours, tossing around and getting in and out of bed, and pacing around the room.

None of my company paid much attention to the fracas—out of politeness, I guess, because surely they could hear it all—but Marilyn followed me out to the kitchen.

"What was the matter?" she said.

"Wasn't it awful! I could die!"

"Oh, well . . ." She shrugged. "Mostly it was just loud."

"My Aunt May was mad about something."

"What?"

"I don't know." I did, though, a little bit, because I'd heard Mother go into the bedroom and try to talk to Aunt May. "Now, May," she had said, "you and I know what the matter is, but I can't shut off all Janet's good times because you're having a bad time. They're just young girls and they're happy, and you wouldn't mind it all so much if you'd just find some happiness in your own life . . . or at least recognize it when you've got it."

I didn't know exactly what that meant, but I *could* figure out that it wasn't the noise that Aunt May found unbearable.

For the rest of that week, while Peggy Watkins was visiting at Marilyn's house, we stayed glued to her side, hoping to pick up some tips or hints or feminine wiles or *something* to use on Eddie Walsh, but Peggy's mind was on stephanotis bouquets and pressure cookers.

We asked her how she had caught Howard's eye in the first place but she said it hadn't been like that at all; that she had never even noticed Howard until one day when they happened to meet at the bank, and then they noticed each other and that was that. This was no help at all to us—we had been noticing Eddie Walsh, up hill and down dale, for six months.

"There must have been more to it than that," Marilyn said later. "Maybe he thought she was rich . . . they met at a bank, she said."

But neither one of us believed that, or thought for one minute that romance had anything to do with money. If you were already very rich, we assumed, you would probably fall in love with somebody else who was very rich, but only because you would move in rich circles and only know rich people.

"Maybe she had on a new dress," I said, "or a new hairdo or new shoes, and didn't really look any different or any better, but just felt terrific about herself . . . you know?" We had both experienced the magic of feeling beautiful and on top of the world because we were wearing a new pink sweater, or because our hair turned out exactly right for a change.

"Maybe," Marilyn mused, without much conviction.

I don't know why we were so determined to establish cause and effect, except that Peggy's experience (knowing Howard, seeing him here and there for a long time, and then suddenly . . . *Wham!*) so exactly paralleled our own: we knew Eddie Walsh, saw him all over the place at school and the youth group and the A&P, and therefore concluded that it might someday be *Wham!* for us, too.

So we drove ourselves and Peggy crazy, and when she left with her family on Saturday, she must have been delighted to see the last of us.

By Saturday, too, Aunt May and I were back on civil terms, having been extremely cool and distant with each other since the night of the party. I had halfway planned to maintain this attitude all summer, but it quickly got to be too much of a chore—remembering to act hurt and put-upon all the time—especially since no one, including Aunt May, paid any attention.

Besides, Marilyn and I were now engaged in a stringent, time-consuming program of self-improvement. Mother, thinking that meant that we were going to read a lot of long hard books and maybe teach ourselves conversational French, was all for it . . . and all wrong.

Chapter Two 🌿

What we were out to improve was, quite literally, our selves: our bodies, our hair, our fingernails . . . we hoped in time for the youth retreat, for which we had such lofty romantic expectations. We had never participated in a youth retreat and consequently those expectations were based on unofficial underground information from a girl named Betty Lou Fultz. The *official* line, set forth by the assistant minister, described it as "a time of renewal and refreshment; a time to get in touch with yourself and examine your priorities and your life choices." But Betty Lou, who had been on last year's retreat, told us, "You're out in the middle of nowhere with all these neat boys, and everyone pairs up with someone. It's terrific!"

Obviously it would be more terrific if you were thin and pretty and all pulled together than if you weren't, and though neither of us was in *terrible* shape, we felt there was room for improvement.

We began with a scientific approach to sun-tanning. At ten o'clock every morning we spread a blanket in the side yard, put on our bathing suits, and slathered ourselves with a mixture of baby oil and vinegar, and set my father's Big Ben alarm clock to ring every fifteen minutes. We kept at it till four-thirty in the afternoon and started again the next morning, revolving from back to side to front to side to back, on signal from the alarm clock.

My grandmother said it didn't look decent, but Mother said it wasn't the looks of it that she minded; what she minded was the smell of the vinegar and the jumpy sensation of waiting, all day long, for an alarm clock to ring every fifteen minutes.

The weather was bright and hot and sunny so we were getting good results (sharp lines of white under our rings), but after two and a half days of this we were also getting bored stiff, and when Pansy appeared with a ball in her mouth we jumped at the chance to sit up for a while and do something different.

Pansy mostly ran around in circles, though, like a small white mechanical toy, dropping the ball and picking it up again, as if she didn't care whether we played with her, but wanted to be where we were while she played by herself. But then Pansy would never chase a ball or a stick or fetch a newspaper. She only chased things nobody could see—a bug, a leaf, a sunbeam.

That day she chased something—maybe a fly, maybe a puff of dust—across the street and straight into the path of a car.

She hit the grille and fell under the wheels and just lay there, almost before we knew what had happened. The driver got out of the car and ran around the front of it to look at Pansy and then, with his face white and his hands shaking, he came to speak to us—Marilyn and me in our bathing suits, smelling of vinegar, too horrified to say a word.

Mother came running down the back stairs and across the yard and then she stopped before she ever got to Pansy and just stood there, staring at the man. "Why. . .Cramer. . ." she said. "Cramer. . . . What in the world . . . ?"

"Jane?" He stared too, shaking his head. "I didn't even think about this being your house, it's been so long. I had no idea . . . I was just . . . and now I've . . ." He gestured toward the street. "I've run over your dog. The dog just ran out from nowhere . . ."

"Oh, poor Pansy!" Mother stepped into the street. "Oh, the poor thing!"

"I'm just as sorry as I can be . . ."

"Oh, I know you are, Cramer. I know that. These things just happen, that's all. We never like to keep her tied, but she *would* run out that way . . ."

This Cramer—the name rang a bell but I didn't yet remember who he was—picked Pansy up and carried her to the yard. "I'll take her to a doctor if you want me to, Jane, but I don't think there's much point."

There wasn't—anyone could see that—so we got the blanket and put it over Pansy. Marilyn was crying, which irritated me. It seemed that if anyone was going to cry it should be me, but I was a delayed reactor when it came to tears. Later that day, maybe not till the middle of the night, I knew that I would suddenly think of Pansy running around the house, skittering on throw rugs, chasing dust motes in the air . . . and then I would bawl my eyes out. But not yet.

I suppose Aunt May saw it all as soon as she turned the corner—the car stopped in the middle of the road, all of us standing around the yard, maybe even the little bundle that was Pansy. She had been to the grocery store and had a sack in her arms, but she just dropped the sack where she was and came full speed ahead down the street, calling as she came, "What is it? What's happened?"

As soon as I saw Aunt May I remembered who Cramer must be because there couldn't be that many first-name Cramers, and Aunt May had been married to one and divorced, while I was still a baby. He was her first husband, and his name was Cramer Gentry, and I'd never heard another thing about him until today, when he showed up out of nowhere and drove down our street and ran over our dog.

Aunt May stopped absolutely short as soon as she got close enough to identify the cast of characters, and just stood there, staring first at Cramer Gentry, and then at Pansy's remains underneath the blanket.

It was a crazy situation, like a jigsaw puzzle put together wrong with all the pieces fitting but the picture cockeyed. You wanted to think about Pansy and what had happened to her and feel sad about that, but you also wanted to know what Aunt May was going to do, suddenly coming face to face with her first husband.

And then there was Cramer Gentry, who we later learned was just driving through town on his way to Cincinnati on business. He was obviously upset about the dog and wanted to do the right thing about that, and here he was suddenly confronted with people out of his past, including a wife.

Surely the greatest mix of emotions fell to Aunt May. She adored Pansy—fed her, petted her, talked to her, took her to bed, walked her three or four times a day . . . had, in fact, gone to the grocery store specifically for chopped meat to tempt Pansy's lagging summer appetite. All other considerations aside, she would have sat right down on the ground and picked up Pansy, blanket and all, and keened over her with all the abandon of the women we read about in Greek plays . . . crying Woe and tearing their garments.

But of course she couldn't do that because she was also struck dumb by the sight of a husband she hadn't seen in twelve or thirteen years.

As I saw it, all the courses of action open to her were bizarre: she couldn't, in one and the same breath, mourn over Pansy and inquire what Cramer had been doing with himself for the last twelve years; it would be humanly impossible to ignore Cramer and concentrate on Pansy; and, for Aunt May, equally impossible to ignore Pansy—dead, under a blanket—for any reason at all.

Fortunately, everyone began to talk at once—Mother, telling Cramer how fond Aunt May was of the dog; Aunt May, telling me to go and call the vet; Cramer, telling Aunt May that it was no use, the dog was dead, and how sorry he was.

"And where in this world did you come from?" Aunt May said to him. "After all these years to show up here . . . and poor Pansy . . ." Then her face crumpled and her eyes filled up with tears and she began to cry, which she did the way she did everything else—without restraint or reserve or any concern about what people might think.

She wanted to bury Pansy then and there, and sent me for a shovel, and argued with Mother when Mother pointed out that there was no place *to* bury Pansy. "Go in and call the police," Mother told me quietly. "Tell them what's happened and ask for someone to come and take the dog away."

We went, not at all sure of the outcome. We had been sent for a doctor, a shovel, and now the police, which seemed like an orderly, if grim, progression of requirements. As we were going up the back steps there was a loud, insistent clanging from the yard—the alarm clock.

"Oh!" Marilyn said. "I set it just before—you know, before it happened." She stared at me. "It's only been fifteen minutes."

I knew just how she felt . . . it seemed like an hour.

The police came and took Pansy, and almost had to take Aunt May too because she wouldn't hand over the dog. She wouldn't take back the blanket either.

"Well, but lady, you'll want to keep your blanket," one of the officers said.

"What are you going to put her in?" Aunt May demanded, and when they didn't produce anything, she personally laid Pansy, still wrapped up, on the backseat of the police car.

Of course it was Mother's blanket, and part of our sun-tanning equipment, but I didn't really care because I thought Aunt May was right, and maybe Mother did too.

When they had left, Mother told us to go in and wash off the vinegar and put on some clothes, and she asked Cramer Gentry if he wouldn't like to come in too and have a cool drink. But he said no, that he was due in Cincinnati.

Then he said good-bye and shook hands all around

with everyone except Aunt May. He didn't seem to know what to do about Aunt May, and finally just said, "Well, May, it was good to see you again," which shook me to my bootheels, it seemed so feeble a parting sentiment under the circumstances.

Aunt May watched him drive away down the street, squinting her eyes in the sun. "Did you have any chance to talk?" she asked Mother. "What did he have to say for himself?"

"Well, May, it wasn't what you'd call a conversational visit."

"I just wonder why he drove by here. Seems like a funny way to drive through town."

Mother hesitated briefly. "There's a detour down on the Trail where they're laying new sewer pipe. He had to come this way."

"Oh." Aunt May fished in her pocket for a cigarette, still looking off down the street. "Well. Cramer Gentry. Did he say where he's living now? What he's doing? I suppose he's married."

"Yes," Mother said. "He mentioned something about his wife. He's married."

Marilyn and I spent most of the afternoon speculating about Aunt May and Cramer Gentry and their marriage and marriage in general.

"She got married again too, didn't she?" Marilyn said. "Who was he? Did you know him?"

"His name was Jim Huddleston. I hardly ever saw him . . . they lived in St. Louis."

"Maybe your Aunt May didn't like St. Louis," Marilyn said.

Neither one of us could make any sense out of Aunt May's matrimonial tangle. You fell in love, you planned a wedding, friends gave you sheets and towels and pots and pans, and you got married . . . like Peggy Watkins. That was the way we saw it, and we accepted, as an article of faith, the presence of destiny in marriage: whoever you happened to marry would automatically turn out to be exactly the person you *should* have married. And yet . . . Aunt May.

I suppose Mother knew what we were talking about, out in the backyard swing, and decided we should hear some plain truth. She came out with a plate of cookies and worked her way around to the subject.

"I guess you don't remember Cramer Gentry," she eventually said. "He was married to your Aunt May a long time ago but it didn't work out."

"Why not?" I asked.

"Well . . ." She dusted her hands together. "I'll just tell you why not, you and Marilyn, and you try to remember it. It was because they didn't put their heads into the marriage, only their hearts. You have to work at a marriage just like anything else, and you have to be *willing* to work at it. Your Aunt May never seemed to take that in, and when there came three days in a row that weren't absolutely wonderful, she just . . ." Mother stopped and cleared her throat, not wanting to kick Aunt May when she was down, I guess. "They were probably too young."

That was a good, safe, standard pronouncement but it was not, I felt, the whole story.

I got a few more cryptic clues that evening while I dried the pots and pans at the kitchen sink. My father had gone out back to water the lawn, which he did every night after supper . . . and Mother had gone out back to tidy up the flower garden, which she did every night after supper. It never occurred to me that they did this to get away from Grandma, Aunt May, and me, and have a chance to talk to each other.

I could hear them through the open kitchen window. ". . . could hardly believe my eyes," Mother was saying, "though he looks pretty much the same."

"That's a good trick, after twelve years," my father said.

"Oh, he looks older of course, but he's not bald or overweight or gray. That's what I mean."

"Always liked Cramer . . . good solid man."

"But May . . . well, May wanted to believe that he had driven past here just in the hope of seeing her," Mother went on. "After twelve years! Imagine! And of course no such thing ever entered his mind."

My father said no, of course not. "You don't think she'll take it into her head to go after Cramer again?"

"Why, no, how could she? He's married."

"Well, so is this man in Detroit, you told me. May

might just decide it's Cramer she's wanted all along."

"Oh, I don't think so. I don't know *what* May wants—May doesn't know herself. To her, the grass is always greener on the other side of the fence, till she *gets* to the other side of the fence and finds out that all the grass is pretty much the same. That kind of thing is easier to take when you're young." I looked out the window to see her put her arm through his. "You know, you're a good solid man yourself, to put up with all this. . . . Don't forget to water my petunias, will you."

"No." My father sighed. "Surely does seem strange not to have Pansy running through the water and chasing fireflies."

That did it, for me. I forgot all about Aunt May in the pathos of remembering Pansy and I stood for ten minutes, wiping one pan and crying my eyes out.

The next day was Sunday, a perfectly ordinary Sunday, which I spent in the usual way without ever knowing what was in store for me.

Later, I would find that incredible, and would try to pretend that I had had a hunch, a happy premonition . . . because Marilyn and I believed in that kind of psychic sorcery: if, by accident, we both wore yellow sweaters to school on the same day, it meant that something good was going to happen; if we failed to do the English homework, and there was a substitute who didn't know anything about the assignment, we took that as a credit to our personal ESP.

But I had no ESP about that remarkable Sunday—
just as well, certainly, for I would have been a basket
case all day.

My father never seemed to remember, from one
week to the next, about the Youth Fellowship, so he
was always surprised to see me dressed up and going
out on Sunday evening. In our town everything closed
down on Sunday, and I guess he knew I wouldn't
get dressed up just to walk to Marilyn's house.

"Where's Janet going?" I heard him ask my mother,
as I came down the stairs.

"To the Methodist church, to their young people's
group." She laughed. "That's where she goes every
Sunday. I don't know why you can't remember that."

"I suppose I can't remember it because I don't understand it. Why doesn't she go to her own young
people's group if she's going to go to one? What do
the Methodists have that's so wonderful, Janet?"

What the Methodists had, of course, was Eddie
Walsh.

"Nothing," I said. "It's just that that's where everyone goes."

"You surely aren't going to leave now," Mother
said. "It doesn't take any hour to walk to the church."

But it did, almost—Marilyn and I always allowed
ourselves lots of extra time so we could walk very,
very slowly and not get rumpled or sweaty or have
our hair blow around.

"What if he isn't there tonight?" Marilyn said. She

said this every single Sunday—something on the order of a death wish, I thought.

"He's always there."

"Sometimes I have this nightmare," she said, "that
I've washed my hair and put it up on rollers and
that I'm wearing that old pink chenille bathrobe that
looks like a bedspread, and I go to the door and it's
Eddie Walsh with a box of groceries from the A&P."

"Marilyn, the A&P doesn't deliver."

"I *said* it was a nightmare. But . . . *br-r-r.*" She
shivered.

To be honest, the Youth Fellowship meetings were
pretty dull—games or skits, or lectures on how to
be halfway decent and still have a good time, or movies—but they were never so all-out churchy as to put
people off. Of course nothing would have put Marilyn
and me off as long as Eddie was there, but we certainly
preferred movies to sermons—even such movies as
these: *A Little Journey Through Jerusalem* . . . *Flowers
of the Bible* . . . *Fruits of the Earth*, which surprisingly,
turned out to be a kind of wine commercial.

Afterward there was discussion, but never very
much, and lots of refreshments, and then everybody
left to go home or walk downtown or just hang around
outside, the way you do on summer evenings.

We stood around that night too, trying to look casual and saying things like "I liked the wine movie
better" and "We really ought to go"—as if we were
just getting a breath of air before going on to some
exclusive celebration.

Marilyn went back into the church to get her sweater and suddenly, without a thunderclap or an earth tremor or even an icy tingle up and down my spine, there beside me was Eddie Walsh.

"ComeonI'llwalkyouhome," he muttered . . . just like that, all six pearly words strung together.

I had rehearsed all kinds of remarks and replies to make to Eddie Walsh on almost any occasion: should I meet him on the bus; should I find his wallet, his geometry book, his blue sweater; should I faint, unexpectedly, in front of his house.

But I had never thought up what to say in reply to "ComeonI'llwalkyouhome"—such preparation being on a par with learning to curtsy in case I ever found myself before the Queen of England. So I didn't say anything at all. Not Yes, or Okay, or I'd love to . . . maybe I nodded my head but probably not.

I just fell into step beside him, expecting, every second, to wake up; half afraid that I had drifted from fact into fancy, and that behind my back everyone was saying, "Look at Janet, what's she doing? What's wrong with her?"

I did look back once to see if I could catch Marilyn's eye . . . and indeed I could. She was standing on the steps of the church, mouth open, eyes wide, sweater dragging.

"See you later?" I called, and she nodded her head six or seven times very fast, up and down . . . which I took to mean, "Call me up the minute you get inside the door of your house!"

He walked me home, and I felt the whole way exactly the same as when I had bronchial pneumonia: dizzy, hot, shaky, and on the thin edge of delirium. By the time we got to Taylor Road, halfway home, Eddie had said three things, none of which I'd heard, and I had said two things, both of them "Pardon me?" I didn't dare say Pardon me? again for fear he would think I was stone deaf instead of (hopefully) just too self-assured to care about conversation.

Somewhere along Taylor Road he linked his arm in mine and took my hand—a piece of business which had figured in many a dream. In dreams, it was fine . . . but in fact it was uncomfortable and tense and sweaty. In no time at all my arm went numb, and then all pins and needles, and then cramped.

Eddie said something which, again, I didn't hear, and this was ultimate torture . . . for who knew what he might be saying? Or what I ought to say in reply? If he was telling jokes I wanted to laugh; if he was asking me for a date I wanted, for heaven's sake, to say yes; if he was just talking about the weather I wanted to agree that it was hot or cold or going to rain . . . but nothing seemed safe to say.

We reached the house and without his asking, or my suggesting, we went around to the backyard swing. And there we sat for over forty-five minutes in absolute silence, holding hands and, eventually, kissing . . . despite a resolution Marilyn and I had made about not kissing anybody on a first date, when we ever had one.

But this resolution was based on the assumption that we would know and be on a friendly basis with whoever it was we were dating and kissing, or not kissing. I didn't really know Eddie Walsh. He was not a friend, but an object of adoration—I just about had to kiss him because I didn't know what else to do, or what in the world to talk about.

What I really needed was for someone to turn on the porch light or come out and water the lawn or, in any way at all, put a stop to this romantic adventure so I could go in and call Marilyn and then go someplace private, dark, and quiet and relive the whole thing.

It occurred to me that this was just about the time Aunt May always took Pansy out for a walk, except that Pansy . . . Emotions being so mixed and tangled—tears of joy, giggles of embarrassment—I knew that I was about to cry for the death of Pansy and the heaven of kissing Eddie Walsh. And out of fear that he would think I was stark staring mad as well as deaf, I finally found my tongue and said, "I think I'd better go in."

Maybe he was relieved. He didn't object, anyway, but said, "Okay," and kissed me one last time. I took a chance and opened my eyes so I could remember, later, how he looked while kissing, but all I could see was his earlobe which was not his best feature . . . or anyone's, when you think about it.

We stood up and walked around to the corner of the house. Perversely, I would have liked to start all over again but he squeezed my hand and said, "So long," and started off. At the edge of the grass he turned and said, "You be home Wednesday night?"

Would I be home? For Eddie? Barring the end of the world . . . yes.

I said "Sure" and he said "I'll see you" and then he walked away down the street, wiping the lipstick off with a handkerchief.

I stood by the porch railing for three or four minutes—hung on to the porch railing actually, because I felt so weak and boneless and feverish and exalted. And then, while the whole thing was still crystal clear in my mind, I raced for the telephone, only to find it in use.

Our telephone stood on a spindly little table by the stairs—room there for one person, so three looked like a mob: Mother, my father, Aunt May.

"I won't let you do it, May," Mother was saying, "Where's your pride? And what's the point?"

I saw then that Aunt May had the telephone and was clutching it to her.

"Put the telephone down," my father said. "Next thing, you'll pull it right out of the wall, fighting over it."

Mother grabbed for the phone. "I won't have her call that man on my telephone! What if his wife should answer?"

"I'll hang up," Aunt May said. "His wife never knew anything about me. What do you think I want to do?"

"I know what you want to do," said Grandma, from the living room. "You want to carry on with a married man and pretend that he isn't a married man, and that you're not carrying on!"

"I do not," Aunt May said, and her eyes filled up with tears. "I just want . . . I just want to talk to him for a minute. . . ."

It all sounded very dramatic and at any other time I would have been interested, but right now I was just crazy to talk to Marilyn. "I want to use the telephone," I said.

"Later, later . . ." My father waved me upstairs in what was for him a very abrupt manner, so I went. "Now I've had just about enough of this," I heard him say. "How do you think this looks to her . . . grown people standing around yelling at each other and struggling over a telephone. Now, May, put that telephone down and for once in your life count to ten . . ."

I went into my mother's room and shut the door and hunched there on the bed in the dark, hanging on to the evening's experience. Why me, I wondered? Why tonight? Had Eddie been waiting all these weeks to catch me alone, without Marilyn? Or had he just suddenly—like Peggy Watkins' Howard—noticed me, glowing with self-improvement suntan? Had I said or done anything special that evening to catch his eye and fancy? And if so, what? . . . so that I could say it or do it on a regular basis for the rest of my life. Or was he looking ahead to the youth retreat at which, according to Betty Lou, there was all that pairing off, and many clandestine meetings in the woods between the girls' and the boys' dormitories?

Out of all these possibilities I chose to believe that Eddie had been watching me for some time with interest, could no longer resist my charms, and planned to claim me for the whole retreat.

Believing this, I could also believe that my mother would say, "Yes, yes, of course go to Lake Clement with the group," although she had actually said nothing more firm than "I don't think so, but we'll see," which was exactly what Marilyn's mother had said.

Marilyn . . . I positively itched to call her, although the conversation would have to be a cautious one. I would have to hint, and she would have to surmise, which would drive both of us crazy.

As it turned out there was no conversation at all. By the time my father talked Aunt May out of making her phone call it was almost midnight and I knew perfectly well that no one was going to let me call Marilyn at midnight without a lot of explanation.

Instead I got into the rollaway bed and propped my pillow in the window frame and leaned my head against the screen . . . from which neck-wrenching position I could see a little piece of the backyard swing and a little piece of the moon, and could feel myself a part of the whole soft summer night.

Chapter Three 🌿

I didn't expect to go to sleep—not with every nerve end vibrating—and was therefore surprised when I woke up. Surprised, too, that the backyard swing looked just the way it always did in the morning sun—old, creaky, and in need of paint. It had no special radiance today. Neither was I transfigured, except for the sharp imprint of the window screen still on my forehead.

My father said, at breakfast, that maybe I shouldn't wash my face—somebody might want to play tiny tick-tack-toe on me. He seemed very jolly, despite last night's telephone rumpus; Mother and Grandma, not; Aunt May was absent from the scene.

"Marilyn called," Mother said, "at *seven o'clock* this

morning. She seemed to think you'd be awake at that hour. Something very important, she said."

The air was heavy with everyone waiting to hear what was important enough to get Marilyn out of bed at seven o'clock, and I decided to take a chance on killing two birds with one stone. "That must mean her mother said she could go on the retreat," I said. "So if she can go, it's all right for me to go, isn't it?"

"Oh, I don't know," Mother said. "I don't know about that retreat. I don't know any of the people in charge, or any of the people going . . ."

"When is this retreat?" my father asked.

"The third week in August. But they have to know how many people are going, so you have to sign up."

"Well . . ." He stirred his coffee round and round. "I think that might be a very good thing. Be a nice change. Everybody needs a change now and then."

I knew perfectly well what he was thinking—that with Aunt May running wild here at home, and apt to run wilder, I would be a whole lot better off at a church retreat where, presumably, all the stress would be on wholesomeness.

My mother continued to frown a little—I guess she suspected there was more to this than renewal and refreshment—but she didn't often put her foot down when my father didn't.

"Then I'd better call Marilyn back," I said, "because she'll want to know."

It was a cryptic conversation. "I can go," I said, conscious of all the listening ears.

"Go where? What are you talking about? What happened last night?"

"Since your mother said you could go on the retreat, I can go too."

"My mother said . . ." She stopped, and I could almost hear her mind working, grinding away. "Oh. Oh! . . . So I'll tell my mother . . . Oh . . ."

"And listen," I went on, "why don't you come over?"

"Of course I'm coming over!"

Now was the time when I really needed my room: a place where we could go and shut the door and talk without interruption or fear of interruption. But the door of my room was already closed with Aunt May behind it, and Marilyn and I were driven, for privacy, back to the side yard with a different blanket and the bottle of baby oil.

"Something happened," she said. "What happened?"

"You won't believe it," I told her . . . and when I had finished describing every moment, every thought, every scrap of conversation (no problem there) she drew a deep, shuddering breath and said, "You're right. I wouldn't believe it, if I hadn't seen you walk off with him. Tell me again exactly what he said about Wednesday night."

I did, and we examined the message word by word

to arrive at its intent. Did I have a date? That was my question, for it seemed like such an offhand arrangement.

"Why would he ask if you were going to be home, unless he planned to show up?" Marilyn said. "It isn't as if he was asking you to the senior prom or something. What are you going to wear? What do you think you'll do?"

"I don't know," I said, "and I'm not going to think about it."

She stared at me. "How can you *not* think about it?"

How, indeed? . . . having thought of nothing else for months. I was afraid that Eddie wouldn't appear on Wednesday evening; I was afraid that he would appear, and that I would be so dull or so silly, would find nothing to say or would spend the whole time with my foot in my mouth . . . that he would suddently remember urgent business elsewhere: a sick uncle, baseball practice, home chores—"Gee, I just remembered that I have to wallpaper the hall tonight."

I was afraid that he might want to spend the whole evening, again, in the backyard swing . . . and I was afraid that he wouldn't. I was afraid it would rain and my hair would hang in lanky strings around my ears or, even worse, that my grandmother would run out with an umbrella.

I was afraid he would forget where I lived.

All in all, it seemed that each of those three days was seventy-two hours long, and that Wednesday evening would never come . . . but of course it did.

"There's some boy coming down the street," Aunt May yelled from upstairs. "I think it's the paperboy for his money. Shall I throw down some money?"

The paperboy was Billy Jenkins, twelve years old and fat and grubby. Aunt May, I thought, must need glasses.

"Never mind," I said. "It's a friend of mine. He said he might stop by."

"How much money shall I throw down?" Aunt May yelled again, and Mother went to the foot of the stairs. "It isn't the paperboy, May," she called. "It's a friend of Janet's."

Eddie could hardly miss all this, with the windows and doors open to the evening air, and I hurried out quickly before Grandma could chime in too, from wherever she was.

He had stopped at the edge of the porch and was leaning on the railing, looking up, smiling. I suddenly knew that I had never really expected him to show up . . . and so that was the first thing I said, despite much careful rehearsal of other, more breezy greetings.

"I didn't really think you'd come," I said.

"Yeh? Why not? . . . You said you'd be home." He looked around me, toward the front door. "Did something better turn up?"

"Oh, no!" Too quick, I thought, too eager . . . but then there *wasn't* anything better on the face of the earth.

"Next time I'll write it down on a piece of paper," he said, "or on the back of your hand."

Next time?

"Want to walk downtown . . . see what's going on? I heard the movie was lousy, but . . ."

Next time?

". . . and get a pizza. Okay?"

"Fine," I said. "That's fine. . . . Oh, wait . . . I'd better tell my folks I'm going."

I'm pleased to say that no one ran amok at the news. Who was I going with, they wanted to know, and Mother peeked out the window to see.

"Oh, I know that boy," she said. "He works at the A&P. Is anyone else going?"

"Well, there'll be kids at the pizza place. There always are."

"Yes, I guess so, on a summer evening. And he'll walk you home, will he? And you won't be too late?"

"I won't." I stopped to look in the hall mirror and saw there nothing new and different . . . yet Eddie had said, ". . . next time . . ." How could he know, at this point, that he would ever want to lay eyes on me again?

Despite the suntan and the shiny hair (Marilyn and I not only used vinegar to sunbathe, we also washed our hair in it, requiring my mother to buy it in huge gallon jugs) I hadn't turned into a raving beauty, or anything close. Eddie certainly couldn't have gone home from that first encounter chuckling over my witty repartee because there wasn't any . . . and though I knew several popular girls who were downright homely, and several popular girls who were silent and solemn—Libby McCall, for instance, who wrote long, sad, dust-to-dust poems, and donated *Madame Butterfly* to the school record collection—these girls shared a quality absent in me: great confidence, and a visible satisfaction about themselves. It *took* a lot of confidence, to demand that *Madame Butterfly* be played at an after-school dance.

In the absence, then, of beauty or wit or social ease or wealth (in case Marilyn and I were wrong, and money *could* buy love) or that indefinable magic which made everything work for some girls, what was it that had brought Eddie back, and would, apparently, bring him back again?

I had thought a lot about this since last Sunday night, and could come to only one conclusion: I must be, unbeknownst to myself, a spectacular kisser . . . or, I guess, kissee.

This was something, but it was not what I would choose to be remembered as, because I knew—we all knew, from books and articles and guidance lectures and cautious motherly advice—that no really solid relationship could be formed or sustained on nothing more than hours and hours in the backyard swing.

43

I was, therefore, relieved to discover that this was not what Eddie had in mind; that what he had in mind was simply standard fare for summer dates in the middle of the week—to hang around. Even people with cars would drive their cars downtown and then go someplace to hang around.

Eddie and I walked, that first evening, all over town, stopping to hang around at the places where other people had stopped to hang around: the drugstore, the bowling alley, the pizza place . . . and all these familiar ports of call seemed different—bigger, brighter, shined and spruced up.

Later, I would mention to my mother that Slattery's Drugstore had been redecorated . . . new paint, new tables, new lighting . . . and she would say, "They must have worked pretty fast. I was there at noon today to get your grandmother's liniment, and it looked just the way it always has, right down to last year's calendar on the wall. Not that I blame Frank Slattery; he's certainly not going to buy new tables for you kids to write your names on."

I really thought he had, though, so rose-colored were all sights and scenes to me that evening.

They were unlikely gathering places. The drugstore was, after all, a drugstore, as Mr. Slattery reminded us from time to time when the noise and the press of bodies got to be too much for him. "I'm thinking about taking out all this lunch counter and soda fountain," he said at least once a week, but of course he never did it.

At the bowling alley there was no place to sit down unless you were bowling, and you could never bowl because it was always full of neighborhood leagues . . . and though there was music—an old jukebox—at the pizza place, there was no room to dance . . . and, by the time we got there that evening, hardly any room to sit down. Unlike Mr. Slattery, Mr. Metrakis, who ran the pizza place, kept saying he was going to knock out a wall and put in more tables and booths, but of course *he* never did it either.

We squeezed into a booth with Eddie's friend Joe Cleveland and his girl Linda Salem and two or three others, and they were probably just as surprised to see me there with Eddie Walsh as I was surprised to be there with him. I envied the ease of people like Linda and Joe, who were steady dates and took each other for granted.

"Here, Eddie," Linda said, "you and Janet eat the rest of this pizza. Metrakis got the order wrong and put mushrooms on it and Joe can't eat mushrooms, they make him sick." She sounded like my mother, telling a waiter that there couldn't be any scallops in a seafood thing, because my father couldn't eat scallops.

How close you had to be to a person, I thought, to know what made him sick, and how secure, to announce it in front of everybody.

"Is that a fact?" Eddie said. "I never knew that."

Joe nodded. "They turn me green. But what I do,

if I get stuck with mushrooms, I just slide them onto Lindy's plate." He grinned.

"Of course, I don't *like* mushrooms," she said. "But what does he care?" She poked him in the ribs and he poked her back and they tussled briefly in the crowded booth, while everybody yelled at them to cut it out.

Around ten-thirty four or five boys came in without dates, fresh from the horror movie, which, they said, wasn't really all that lousy. "Actually, it *is* lousy," one of them said—Coe Brant, another friend of Eddie's, "but it's *so* lousy that it's funny. It has this gorilla who's like maybe two feet tall, with curly fur . . ."

". . . and there's this werewolf that looks like Bob Hope," someone else said, and then they all chimed in with details of the monsters and most of the plot, and finally collapsed, laughing, on tables and chairs.

"Is that a fact?" Eddie said, and looked at me. "I guess we'd better check it out . . . somebody give me a pen or a marker or something." Somebody tossed him a bright green marker and he wrote on the back of my hand, *Friday 7:30.* "Okay?"

"Eddie, that's awful," Linda said. "She'll have to scrub and scrub to get it off."

This was good news to me because of course I didn't want to get it off, and if what Linda said was true, it might hold up through two or three weeks of normal washing.

It was almost eleven o'clock when we started home,

walking slowly, talking. That was a remarkable thing too, it seemed to me—that there *was* conversation.

"What am I going to talk about?" I had said to Marilyn, who was all sympathy and no help.

"Oh, boy, I don't know. All the magazine articles say it's easy—you just talk about *him*, what he likes and what he does. Maybe you could talk about the A&P."

Oddly enough, we did. Eddie said it was an okay job; I said my mother bought all her meat there. We talked about pizza too—plain cheese versus everything—and we talked about the movie with the two-foot-tall gorilla.

This is small talk, I thought—I'd never known exactly what that was. My mother said it allowed you to converse with people you'd never seen before and might never see again, which was not a happy thought. Mother also said she wasn't very good at it. I didn't know whether I was any good at it or not, but at least we weren't proceeding in paralyzed silence.

And then a little white dustmop of a dog ran out from somebody's house and barked and barked and barked at us, and I said, "Oh, that's just like Pansy," . . . and I found myself telling Eddie about Pansy—her life and times, and how she died, and how awful that was.

"Right in front of you?" he said. "Oh, wow! I had a dog get killed once, but I wasn't there. Good thing,

I guess, that I wasn't. I was only seven years old."
He put his arm around me. "I'm sorry, Janet. That
was rough."

Before I knew it, we were home, and as we walked
around the side of the house I could see my father
in the living room, watching the evening news,
Grandma dozing in one chair, and Mother in another.
I would have *liked* to see Aunt May too, lest she turn
out to be roaming around in the night as she sometimes did . . . or even sitting out in the backyard
swing, contemplating the moon and the stars and her
own checkered career. But then I saw a low light
upstairs in what used to be my room, and heard a
radio playing softly, Aunt May's favorite dreamy, late-
night music.

It seemed more natural to me, this time, to be sitting
in the backyard swing, with Eddie's arm around me,
and to be kissing him . . . but I still had the feeling
that some dizzy fairy godmother, in a hurry, had
grabbed her wand and touched the wrong Cinderella.

The evening ended too soon, in my view . . . and,
Eddie said, in his—". . . but I have to be at work
at seven in the morning."

Instantly, I invested him with all the virtues that
implied—energy, ambition, responsibility. "You
should have told me," I said. "We could have come
home earlier."

He hugged me. "No way." . . . and to the music
of *that* I floated, about six inches off the ground, to

the corner of the porch where we stood in the shadows and said good night.

I watched him walk away, comparing, as best I could, my feelings now with my feelings the last time. I had felt, then, like the people in cartoons who stick a finger in a wall socket and are electrified—hair standing on end, sparks flying off in all directions, buzzing and tingling from head to toe.

This was better, this warm glow, as if Eddie still had his arms around me. It was as pervasive and sweet as the smell of my mother's petunias, planted all around the house.

"What's that great smell?" he had said, and when I told him, "*My* mother's petunias don't smell like that."

"It's because these are white," I said. "White petunias smell the best. White roses, too. My mother says what doesn't go to color goes to smell."

"Is that a fact?" He'd picked one, then, and tucked it behind my ear . . . and when I went in the house I put the petunia in a jelly glass, and perched it on the windowsill behind my rollaway gypsy bed.

Everyone else was down for the night, but Mother heard me, and came out to kiss me good night, and said, "I'm glad you had a good time."

"How do you know I did?"

She smiled and nodded at the petunia. "You'd hardly save a flower to remind you of a bad time, would you?"

She'd always said, whenever I complained of being unlovely and unloved, that I shouldn't be in such a hurry, my time would come, and I guess she thought it had, and was pleased for me.

Chapter Four ✣

Linda was wrong about the green marker. By the next afternoon most of it had faded away, though Marilyn insisted she could read it. "F . . . T . . . no, that's an R. And here's a T . . . no, that's a Y. Well, anyone would know that says Friday."

"I *told* you it said Friday."

"I mean, even if you hadn't." She stared at my hand. "He did that so you wouldn't *forget*? What made him think you might forget?"

"What I said, I guess . . . about not really thinking he would show up."

"Oh, boy." She shook her head. "It almost makes you think they're right, that honesty *is* the best policy. I would never have thought to say that."

"Marilyn, I didn't think to say that! If I'd *thought*, I'd have said almost anything else."

Beyond discussing the back of my hand, and where Eddie and I had gone, I didn't offer any other details and Marilyn didn't ask for any . . . which may be one reason why she's my best friend.

Instead, we talked about her upcoming role as bridesmaid in Peggy Watkins' wedding. We were sitting in the kitchen, driven there by a shower which had settled down to soaking rain, and to my surprise my mother came and sat down too with a cup of coffee.

"What color is your dress, Marilyn?" she asked. "Do all the girls wear the same color?"

"No, they're all different. Mine's yellow . . . that sunny yellow."

"Buttercup," Mother said. "Buttercup yellow." I noticed that she held her mouth a certain way, almost as if she could taste that color, and liked it.

"I guess so." Marilyn looked out the window and sighed. "I planned to have a really terrific tan to go with it . . . and now look at the rain!"

"Oh, Marilyn!" Mother laughed. "It hasn't rained for three weeks, and we need it. Besides, I like a rainy day. Of course, not for weddings, so I hope it doesn't rain for Peggy's wedding. You know what they say, happy the bride the sun shines on."

I had a sudden thought. "Did it rain on Aunt May's wedding day?"

"Why, I don't remember . . . Yes, I do, too. It was in October, and it was a lovely fall day. Very warm."

I wanted to ask which of her weddings that was, but thought better of it.

"But it rained on *my* wedding day," Mother said.

"Oh . . . What did you do about your dress?" Marilyn asked.

"I just wore it." Mother smiled. "It wasn't much of a problem because it wasn't a very big wedding. No one had these big weddings then. May stood up with me, and your Uncle George stood up with Daddy, and when it was over we had a small reception in the social hall of the church. Didn't even know it *was* raining till we stepped outside."

I had never known all this—not that there was much there to know. "What did you wear?" I asked.

"Well . . . *I* thought I had on a white summer dress with a full skirt to my ankles, and a little embroidery around the neck . . . but according to the newspaper it was . . ." She tilted her head a little, as if trying to remember. ". . . oh, yes . . . it was 'striking in its fresh simplicity, with bouffant skirt, and bodice . . .' something or other about embroidery in a petal and vine motif.

"Then there was another whole paragraph about my bouquet, which was nothing in the world but your grandmother's White Dawn roses, a little bit of asparagus fern, and some grape ivy we pulled off the side of the house."

She laughed again—probably at our faces, since we both found this a dampening recital of what ought to be very romantic details. "They surely made it sound a lot more impressive than it was . . . but it was impressive enough for me. Now I'm going across the street to pin up a skirt hem for Hazel Wheeler, if anyone wants to know, and I'll be back by and by."

"I went to a kitchen shower for Peggy last week," Marilyn said, "and everyone there kept saying that same thing about the sunshine—happy the bride the sun shines on! . . . happy the bride the sun shines on! . . . I think I'll tell Peggy not to count on it. Because look at your mother—she got married in the rain, with no fanfare and a homemade bouquet, and everything turned out fine for her. But the sun was shining all over your Aunt May, and it didn't do her a bit of good. . . . Is she going to live here all the time now?"

"Oh, no."

"I wonder what she's going to do. Maybe she'll get married again."

"Maybe she ought to pick a rainy day next time," I said.

A few minutes later Aunt May herself walked in, with a sack full of cosmetics and a face to match.

"I was in the department store," she said, "and there was a salesman there demonstrating a new line of makeup. What do you think?" She studied herself in the kitchen mirror. "The girl told me I was a good subject. Of course, she wanted me to buy all the makeup, which . . ." She emptied the sack out all over the table, and laughed. ". . . I did. I only bought the small sizes though, and I didn't buy the wrinkle cream or the super-enriching hormone lotion, or any of those things." She looked at Marilyn and me, with the critical eye of one who has learned all the secrets and can spot all the flaws. "Do you two want to make yourselves up? I know just what the girl did, and how she did it."

So we spent the rest of the afternoon playing with Aunt May's cosmetics, while she sat at the table, smoking cigarettes and drinking iced tea and telling us how much cream rouge to use, and what color eye shadow to use, and where to put it.

When Mother got back from marking Mrs. Wheeler's hem, Aunt May made her sit down too, to be transformed . . . and even Grandma, scoffing and sniffing about the whole thing, gave in and got what she called a "face-do."

When my father came home he made a big fuss about being in the wrong house, surrounded by beautiful women. He also said that since there was no dinner for him (there wasn't—Mother forgot to put the meat loaf in the oven) he would go out and find some champagne and caviar to go with the elegant company.

What he brought home was Chinese food, which

we demolished . . . although Grandma said she didn't call all that sub-gooey *food*, and she opened a can of beef stew for herself.

"This was a funny day!" Marilyn said later. "I mean, it was a funny day, but it was fun too."

We were cleaning up the kitchen, which we'd volunteered to do—a calculated offer, I'm afraid, since all we had to clean up was a lot of cardboard cartons and Grandma's beef stew pan. Even so, it took a long time, because under Aunt May's guidance, Marilyn had made up one side of her face one way, and the other side another way, and she kept trying to see one side at a time in the mirror.

"I can't decide which looks better for the wedding," she said.

"I don't think Aunt May will let you take all her makeup off to Peggy's wedding." Knowing the ups and downs of Aunt May's nature, I figured we'd be lucky to borrow a lick of lipstick by tomorrow.

"Oh, I'd have to buy my own."

I stood beside her and we looked at ourselves in the mirror. "I guess I won't," she said. "After all, people cry at weddings. I'd have mascara all over my face. But you could wear yours Friday night to the movie. It's not a sad movie."

I didn't, though. I still couldn't figure out what had attracted Eddie to me in the first place, but it certainly wasn't Ripe Wine Creme Blush and smoky eyelids.

Maybe someday, on some big occasion—when we had gone together for so long that, like Linda with Joe, I would know all Eddie's likes and dislikes, his quirks and fancies—I would show up in full war paint. He might say, "Wow! You look terrific!" and that would be great. Or he might say, "What's all the junk on your face?" and I would say, "It's just for fun, just for this one dance . . . this one party . . . this one occasion . . ." and he would humor me, put up with it . . . as you *do* put up with things in the people you care for.

We met Linda and Joe at the movie, and met other people we knew—almost everyone, in fact, in couples and crowds. I saw Marilyn across the lobby, with Beth Huckabee and Kristen Couch. Most of Eddie's buddies were there—some with dates, some roaming around looking for dates.

Before the lights went down—to the usual wild applause—we could see a scattering of grown-ups here and there, but they were mostly young mothers and fathers with little kids, and huge buckets of popcorn. My mother always said they would have to *pay* her to go to the movies on Friday night, and they would have to pay her a lot.

People without dates were always on the move—changing seats, looking for friends, getting popcorn and Coke and candy. They were the ones who led the boos and hisses for the villains, and the cheers and whistles for the heroes . . . and the standing ovation whenever an usher went down the aisle.

"It looks like a giant game of musical chairs," I said, and Eddie laughed. We were sitting at the back of the theatre, with Joe and Linda in front of us, and though there were people on either side, I was hardly aware of them . . . as if there were a little magic circle drawn just around Eddie and me, sitting there in the flickering darkness.

"Do you want some popcorn or anything?" he asked, and when I said no, he put his arm around the back of the seat and made a place for my head on his shoulder.

We watched the movie and the passing parade of people up and down the aisle and laughed at the Bob Hope werewolf and the cross-eyed vampire . . . and at a notorious clown named Dave Coburn, who went from row to row, taking up a collection "to send this vampire to camp."

"I hope they don't kill off the gorilla," I whispered, toward the end. "I really love the gorilla."

"Is that a fact?" Eddie leaned down and kissed me. "Well, he's a lucky gorilla."

I wanted to say, "Of course, I love you too"—bold, but breezy and light and offhand, so he wouldn't know for sure whether I was serious or not. But I knew I couldn't carry that off: the words would dry up in my mouth and come out sounding ponderous and solemn, like testimony in court. I would probably even stammer, and have to clear my throat. It's easier,

I think, to say I love you when you really don't.

Before the movie was over Joe turned around and asked what we were going to do. "I've got the car," he said, "so we can go out to the Colonial and dance, if you want to."

The Colonial, just outside town, was the only place around (except the high school gym) where you could dance, and on Friday and Saturday nights there was a three-piece band, and what they called a "supper menu," which simply meant that kids could go there, get a hamburger and a Coke, and dance for an hour without going broke.

It was always crowded, and that night they'd opened some double doors onto a patio, and filled that up with tables and chairs, and that was where we sat. When the waitress brought our food she brought along a little hurricane candle for the table, but even with that, you couldn't see much.

"This is like a séance," Linda said. "We should all hold hands and ask a question, and I know the very question. The question is, where's the salt? Can anyone see it?"

It *was* dark, but I liked it: all the little flickering lights—each table had its own candle—and the music coming through the open door, and the sound of voices and laughter inside. Joe and Linda went in to dance—"to break a path through," they said—and I was glad we didn't jump right up to follow them.

Eddie held my hand up to the candlelight and traced

the last faint signs of the green marker. "Look, it's almost gone. You must have scrubbed and scrubbed, like Linda said."

"No, it just faded away."

"Well, that's good. You wouldn't want to go around green for life." He was still holding my hand, measuring fingers, and he didn't look at me, just at our hands. "Listen . . . uh, about tomorrow night . . . big Saturday night . . ."

I felt a little chill of premonition, and with it a renewed awareness that this was all really some kind of fairy tale. This wasn't Harold Stepower sitting beside me—fat, earnest, plodding Harold Stepower, whose mother had to drum up dates for him. This was Eddie Walsh, who could point his finger in any direction, anywhere in town, and pick his lady.

Obviously, I thought, he had picked some other lady for tomorrow night, and he was about to tell me that. He might even be about to tell me what a great girl I was, and he would see me around. This was why we hadn't gone in to dance with Joe and Linda . . . did they know? I could feel little trickles of sweat down my side, and I tried to get my face in order so I could smile this very easy, natural smile, and say all the right things.

"The thing is . . ." he began, and I said, "Listen, Eddie, as a matter of fact . . ." and then we both stopped.

"I have to play ball with the town league tomorrow

night," he said. "You wouldn't want to come and watch the game, would you? We can go get a pizza after."

I could actually feel my knees quiver and go weak, and for one awful second I thought that I had forged right ahead with my spur-of-the-moment speech about some big important thing I had to do tomorrow night.

"That's great," I managed to say. "I'd love to."

"Pick you up at seven." He stood up. "Come on, let's go dance."

We found a little patch of floor where no one else was, and danced in that little patch of floor, with Eddie's arm around me and his cheek against mine.

I'd been nervous, earlier, about this—what if I stumbled over my own feet? what if I couldn't follow him? what if they played some South American thing?—but that had given way to a feeling of relief, and to something else . . . the sense that we had crossed some invisible line; that I had gone from being Eddie's date to being Eddie's girl, that we both knew it and that, from now on, everyone else would know it too.

Chapter Five 🌿

Eddie never actually asked me for another date . . . I guess you could say he took me for granted.

All Marilyn's magazine articles tell you that's bad. "Don't always be available," they say. "If he shows up out of the blue, explain that you've made other plans. Suggest that next time he might let you know ahead of time, and include details of the evening's program, what you're going to do, and at what time."

Well, maybe . . . but I don't know anyone who's so loaded up with different boys and dates and places to go and things to do that she has to carry around a little black book and keep a pencil behind her ear. And anyway, being available is almost the whole point, and the best part . . . Eddie could count on me; I could count on Eddie.

I knew that he would show up two or three evenings a week, and he knew that I would be there . . . and my mother got over thinking he should behave like the magazine articles: call me early and make formal arrangments.

"Nobody does that, Mother. Especially in the summertime."

"It's just that when I was a girl . . ." She made a funny little face. "When I was a girl, I swore I'd never say 'When I was a girl . . .' to any child of mine, about anything. But . . ." she sighed, "you do it anyway. Where are you going this evening?"

"To the movies."

We went to movies, and we went to the pizza place and we went to the Colonial to dance to slow moonlight-and-roses music. We went to ball games and we went swimming at the pool.

One silly steamy Sunday afternoon we went looking for neighborhood kids' shows and found three, all offering similar acts; dressed-up dogs, seven-year-old magicians, and comics who told identical jokes— "Now I have a dirty story for you, ladies and gentlemen . . . the pig fell in the mud" and, with many giggles, "How do porcupines make love? . . . Carefully."

Sometimes we went with Joe and Linda, or met them along the way; after ball games we usually ended up with Cliff Hildebrand, who pitched on Eddie's team, and his girl; once we went with a bunch of people to Libby McCall's house to play records . . .

including, of course, *Madame Butterfly.*

More often, though, we just went by ourselves: walked around town, holding hands, or up the hill to the reservoir, with much memorable kissing when we got to the top, where the stars seemed to hang right above our heads.

We laughed about the first time Eddie walked me home, and mumbled so that I couldn't understand him and kept saying, "Pardon me?"

"Yeh, I do that," he said. "Mush-mouth, my mother calls me."

"Why *did* you walk me home that night? I mean . . . you didn't even know my name."

"Sure I knew your name."

"How?"

"Why . . . just the way you know anybody's name." We were sitting in the backyard swing—*I* was sitting in the backyard swing; Eddie was lying down with his head in my lap and his feet hanging over the arm. "I guess I thought you were cute." He studied my face very carefully. "Yeh, that was it all right. I thought you were cute."

"Cute! I'm not cute. You have to be little to be cute."

"Is that a fact?"

"Yes, that *is* a fact."

"What do you mean, little? Do you mean little, five years old . . . or little, five feet tall?"

"Both . . . either."

"Shows you how dumb I am." He sat up, brushed pretzel crumbs from his shirt, and smoothed his hair. "Here all the time I thought you were cute and didn't even know what that was. Well, they say love is blind."

I had realized by now that Eddie, too, couldn't say I love you . . . and so when he said things like this I treasured them, as being the closest he could come. And anyway, I reasoned, he didn't *have* to say I love you—I was just supposed to know he did.

I wasn't the only one in this happy condition— Marilyn, conveniently, had fallen out of love with Eddie. She had been one of four bridesmaids at Peggy Watkins' wedding and in the general kissing that went on there got kissed quite a lot—exclusively, I guess— by Howard's second cousin Jack Kincaid, who lived forty miles away in Massilon.

I heard about all this on the day after the wedding, when Marilyn arrived with her bridesmaid's bouquet, her gift from Peggy—a small jewelry box made to look like a hope chest—and Polaroid pictures of the festivities.

". . . This is Peggy and Howard . . . and Peggy with my mother . . . and here are the bridesmaids, and this is the cake. I brought you a piece. You're supposed to sleep with it under your pillow and who- ever you dream about is who you're going to marry, did you know that? I brought you another piece too, though, to eat. And this is me with Jack."

Jack was short, with sandy-red hair and blue eyes, and he had his arm around Marilyn.

"He was an usher," Marilyn said, "and he was the one I had to walk with back up the aisle, so it wasn't as if he picked me out of the blue . . . although he said he would have anyway. I don't know about that, though."

"Why wouldn't he?" I said. "You look so pretty, Marilyn." She really did—prettier even than Peggy, I thought.

"I think it must have been the yellow dress and the suntan," she said, "but mainly the suntan. That was the smartest idea we ever had, because look what it did for us."

Jack called her every other night and had driven down twice to see her, arriving each time without advance notice, which was exactly what the magazine articles frowned on.

"Well, Marilyn, I hope you explained that you'd made other plans. And I hope you suggested that next time he might let you know."

She shook her head firmly from side to side. "It doesn't count if he comes all the way from Massilon. All the way from Massilon! . . . Jan, do you believe this is us? At the end of school we were just . . . well, whatever we were. Now you're going steady with Eddie Walsh, and I'm going with a boy who drives almost a hundred miles, back and forth, just to see me. It's almost as if we'd sold our souls to the devil."

I knew what she meant. When I was with Eddie, and especially when we were with other people, I didn't have to pinch myself to know it was all true . . . but sometimes I would run into him by accident, or I would see him, unexpectedly, at a distance—walking down the street, or standing on a corner with one of his buddies. And whenever this happened, I always felt the way Marilyn and I used to feel when we spent our days hoping to see him, half afraid we *would* see him (and that he would deduce that we were trailing him all over the place) . . . and always, always, imagining just such a scenario as had happened, now, to me.

"There's a word for that!" Marilyn said. "I read it in a book once. It's French . . . 'déjà vu.' "

I didn't read it in any book, but I recognized the phrase . . . from Aunt May, of all people. I heard her say it the day Pansy was killed—after the police took Pansy, and after Cramer Gentry drove away down the street. "Oh, well," she'd said, almost to herself, ". . . déjà vu . . ."

So much for Marilyn's French, I thought . . . or, maybe, so much for Aunt May's French, because I couldn't see any connection between these two situations.

Summer heat had settled in now with a vengeance, and one hot day melted into the next like wax crayons left in the sun. My mother flew around in the early morning, doing whatever had to be done, and went around again about eleven o'clock, drawing window shades and closing curtains on the sunny side of the house. Aunt May put all her Shalimar perfume in the refrigerator and dabbed herself with it all day long. Iced tea was made by the gallon; meals were prepared two or three at a time and eaten later, cold. The evening air was still and heavy—people couldn't sleep and sat out on their porches and in their yards, and little children in summer pajamas ran around catching lightning bugs in jars.

One evening Eddie and I had walked way down the street and all around the block and back and found my father sitting in the backyard swing.

"Come on and sit down," he said. "I'm about to go in anyway. Not much cooler out than in, but I enjoy the smells of things outside . . . hot sidewalks, after someone's hosed them down. A lot of people hosed them down tonight. And your mother's flowers there—aren't they something! Your mother claims that . . ."

"White flowers smell the best," we both said, at the same time.

"Well!" He laughed. "I guess it must be true then. And this . . ." He reached down to the ground and produced a great big, very red tomato. "Just smell this tomato. That's a beefsteak tomato, came from Joe Wheeler's garden. That's how you tell a good tomato . . . by the smell."

"I never smelled tomatoes," Eddie said.

"Well, now you know to do it. You work at the

A&P, don't you? You just watch and when you see a lady smell the tomatoes . . . and the peaches and the celery and the melons . . . that will be a lady who knows what she's doing." He stood up then, still sniffing his tomato. "Better not stay out here too long. I wouldn't be surprised if we had a thunderstorm."

"I like thunderstorms," I said.

"I like thunderstorms too, but I always worry about that tree. It got struck by lightning once and we almost lost it. If we *did* lose it, we were going to build the porch out farther, so we'd have someplace to hang the swing . . . but it wouldn't be the same."

I hadn't known that, about the tree, and I certainly didn't know that my father thought of the backyard swing as anything special, although of course I did . . . as I thought anything connected with Eddie was special.

My father was wrong about the storm. Despite heat lightning slicing through the sky and far-off thunder rumbles, it didn't rain, and the next day was just as hot and heavy as the days before.

"I believe the world is coming to an end," my grandmother said. "I never remember such heat," . . . and Mother laughed. "You say that every year, and every year's about the same. This summer's no different from any other summer."

But for me it was absolutely different, like going to bed in Ohio and waking up on Mars, where everything you saw or did, and everything that happened, was unlike what had ever been before. Even the smells and sounds and tastes of familiar things seemed remarkably fresh and new—orange juice, the sound of crickets at night, all the smells my father spoke about—and when someone would say, "I'm so bored I could die!" I could hardly remember how that felt.

A lot of people were so bored they could die, including Aunt May, and when midsummer swim night came along, I was half afraid she would go, just for something to do.

"Well, why not?" I heard her say to Mother. "You come and go too. We don't have to swim, but it'll be cool and pleasant to sit there and listen to the music and watch everybody else."

"Oh, May, I'd feel like a fool and you would too. It's for the kids."

It really wasn't exclusively for the kids but that's who went, along with a heavy complement of chaperones. I don't know how or why midsummer swim night ever got started, but it had become an annual event. You could swim, or dance on the concrete apron at the shallow end of the pool; there was music and food all night long; and, in the morning, pancakes and sausage cooked by the Lion's Club. Part of the point was to stay awake and watch the sunrise, and a surprising number of people managed to do that every year.

"Not me," Eddie said. "I've never made it yet."

"Then I think I'll wake you up," I told him, "because you shouldn't miss it. It's the best part."

It always was the best part for me—sitting on a towel, wrapped in a sweat shirt, with whoever else had hung on till dawn . . . seeing the stars blink out, watching the sky turn from black to gray to lavender to pink. There was always someone who said, "I'm going to get up early every day to see this," and there were always people, including me, who made a wish on the last star to go.

Marilyn's wishes were quite specific and concerned problems she didn't really want to tackle on her own: to lose ten pounds, to get all A's. Kristen Couch wished the same thing every year—to inherit or win or find or otherwise come by enough money to visit Paris. People wished for motorbikes or horses or to get their braces off . . . all of which seemed to me like birthday candle wishes and not grand enough for the last star before daybreak.

Consequently my own wishes were vague and fuzzy . . . along the lines of wanting life to be, forever, as pink and promising as a summer sunrise.

And now, of course, it was . . . and there was nothing left to wish except that it would all go on and on and on.

Swim night began at seven o'clock but, traditionally, no one came till nine or nine-thirty, because by then the lights were on, reflected in the water, and the music was playing, and the pool was deep blue-green and shimmery . . . and when you dove in, the water was as soft and warm as the air.

We swam and danced and ate and swam again; threw pennies in the pool and dove for them, and made faces at each other under water. We found Marilyn and Jack Kincaid, who had come down from Massilon for the occasion, and the four of us went around checking on the marathon Monopoly games—a standard feature of swim night.

Around one o'clock there was a last frantic flurry of splashing and throwing people into the pool and water fights and belly-flop dives, and then everything began to quiet down as people fell asleep in spite of themselves.

A few determined swimmers continued to plow up and down the length of the pool, and there were sudden bursts of crackling bright light here and there—leftover Fourth of July sparklers. The Monopoly games were still going on, and would go on into the morning, and behind us in the grass a bunch of people were playing word games—"I'm going on a trip and I'll take a deadly dentist, and an electric elephant, and a . . . a . . . furry Fig Newton . . ." Loud groans, and exclamations of "Ugh . . ." and "Yu-u-ck."

From time to time someone would dive into the pool and you could hear the ripples of water lapping the sides, and from the clubhouse, where the Lions were getting ready to cook breakfast, came the strains of barbershop harmony—someone singing "Lida Rose."

Eddie had fallen asleep beside me on a big beach towel—in our immediate vicinity there were only two people who *hadn't* fallen asleep.

"Well, here we are," Marilyn said, "just like always." She picked her way over and around bodies to where I was. "You know what? Paul Grissom snores. I thought only old people snored. I'd die if I snored . . . I don't, do I? Promise you'll tell me if I ever snore."

"I promise."

"And I'll tell you."

Without even thinking, we linked little fingers and pulled . . . and then laughed at ourselves, automatically following this childish ritual which was supposed to bind your promise through life and death and even through the principal saying "I want you to tell me who wrote this on the blackboard."

"I guess it's like wishing on the last star," Marilyn said. "Maybe we've outgrown that, too . . . what do you think?"

So I don't know whether Marilyn made a wish that night. I didn't, and was to regret it later, but at the time any wish seemed like frosting on the cake.

While it was still dark Marilyn went back to wake Jack, and I woke Eddie, and that was the first thing he said, once he realized what was going on.

"It's still dark!"

"Just barely," I said. "Just barely dark and just barely light. That's what sunrise is, you nut. You have to catch it in a hurry because it's gone so fast."

He got up quickly then, shook himself awake, and pulled me close beside him . . . and we sat there, wrapped in the beach towel, watching dawn break in a wash of rose and gold and purple, spreading up and out till it filled the whole sky.

Eddie said, "Oh . . . Wow! . . ." and shivered a little.

"Isn't it perfect?" I whispered . . . and, behind us, Marilyn echoed that thought, and more.

"Isn't *everything* perfect!" she said. "Isn't everything just perfect!"

I didn't knock on wood when Marilyn said that, but I should, at least, have stopped to think that when you are at the top of the Ferris wheel, you must either go down when it goes, or jump out. You can't stay forever at that peak, suspended in air with all the world spread out below you.

And so, with everything so perfect and all of life so well-ordered and, best of all, bound to go on that way, I got sick—nothing so fleeting as a summer cold, nothing so generally acceptable as mononucleosis. I got poison ivy, and within twenty-four hours I was covered from head to toe: miserable, unlovely, and aware (because of past experience) that I would be this way for a good long time.

Marilyn, who never got poison ivy, had positive

advice. "Just put a bandage over it," she said, over the phone.

"There aren't enough bandages in Slattery's Drugstore," I told her. "It's behind my ears and in my eyebrows . . . and all over my face and my hands. I'm holding this phone in a paper towel."

"Oh-hh," she said. "Oh, Jan . . ."

The main thing on my mind, of course—aside from trying not to scratch—was Eddie.

"Well, just tell him," Marilyn said. "He'll probably bring you flowers or something" . . . but then Marilyn came to keep me company and confirmed what I already knew about myself.

"You look like the picture of Dorian Gray," she said, "after sin had corrupted his countenance. I can understand why you don't want to see Eddie. But what are you going to tell him?"

"I thought you could tell him."

"Tell him what?"

"That I'm sick in bed with something so contagious that nobody's allowed in."

Marilyn said later that it was pretty hard to describe my condition without making it seem that I was at death's door, but she had done her best. "I just said it was some kind of virus, very bad and especially very catching, and that you were in bed and had to stay there, and no one could see you, even me. He was really upset, Janet."

Eddie called that evening, which was a first. He'd

told me that his little sister drove him crazy when he tried to talk to girls on the telephone, so he just didn't try to talk to girls on the telephone, and you could almost tell that from the conversation.

He said he was sorry I was sick, and I said I was too, and there was a long empty pause. I said, "I'm reading this book . . ." and he said, "It was really hot today . . ." which were subjects that Marilyn's magazine articles usually threw in as a last resort—"If conversation lags and all else fails, try books and weather."

It was strange and a little uncomfortable—like talking to an old friend you hadn't seen for a long time—and I was almost relieved when Eddie said, "Listen, I better go. You . . . ah . . . do what they tell you to, okay? Get lots of sleep and all . . ."

"Oh, I will," I said. "I can't help myself. I fall asleep all the time. I went to bed last night at seven-thirty, and didn't wake up till . . ." I stopped. This was my *grandmother's* favorite topic of conversation—sleep; how much, how little, how restless, how deep—and in desperation I said I would have to hang up, that my father wanted to use the phone.

That was the last I heard for four days (a month of days, it seemed) except through Marilyn, who called or came over every day to report on Eddie's whereabouts and activities—she had seen him downtown, she had seen him riding around with Joe Cleveland, she had seen him at the drugstore.

But I wanted total recall, and subtle judgements—what was he doing downtown, and who with? Where was he going with Joe Cleveland? Did he look any different . . . sad, maybe, as if he missed me? Had she heard him say anything like "I haven't seen Janet for five days, seven hours, and thirty-eight minutes?"

I guess I wanted him to feel as cut off as I felt; to be desolate, like Romeo or Heathcliff; to find the days endless and gray, without me . . . and when he called again I wanted him to say those very things, or at least I wanted to hear, in his voice, overtones of those things.

How was I feeling, he wanted to know.

"About the same. What have you been doing?"

"Not much. Not much to do."

Since I was listening for any nuance of despair, I took "not much to do" as evidence of his loneliness—not much to do, without me; life stale and flat, without me; every minute an hour, without me. But then . . .

"Uh . . . there's a party tomorrow night at Linda's house. I guess I'll go to that."

Stung, I said, "Say hello to Linda for me . . . and to Joe. And have a good time."

"Oh . . . well . . . it's no big deal."

I wanted to say "I miss you so much," and knew that I could say that if I were with him . . . but then, of course, it wouldn't make much sense. Perhaps he felt the same way—later, next week, whenever I was up and around and fit to be seen in public, he would tell me just how forlorn a time this had been for him, and I would say, "I know. Me, too" . . . and everything would be all right.

Meanwhile, I was stuck in the house with the heat, the constant whir of electric fans . . . and Aunt May, who seemed as itchy as I felt. It was too hot to go anywhere, she said, too hot even to get dressed. And so she roamed the house in an orange-and-purple wrapper (and nothing else, which my grandmother said would be a fine thing for the milkman to go and tell around).

She got on my nerves, I got on her nerves, we both got on my mother's nerves. Grandma concentrated on my poison ivy and kept me so drenched in calamine lotion that I was sure it would penetrate my pores and leave me chalk white for the rest of my life.

I complained of this, and of boredom, and my appearance, and Aunt May's cat—a stray she had picked up somewhere and brought home. I was forever stepping or sitting on the cat by accident, which made me jumpy and made Aunt May mad.

"For heaven's sake!" Mother said, on one especially touchy day. "Why don't you get dressed and go out somewhere?"

"Go out!" I said. "Mother, look at me!"

"You don't look as bad as you think you do. I don't know whether it's your grandmother's calamine lotion or the doctor's medicine, or what, but it *is* getting better. Look in the mirror."

I did, was unencouraged, and said so.

"Well, it isn't like a twenty-four hour virus, you know—here today and gone tomorrow. My goodness, Janet, you surely don't intend to stay out of sight till every last trace is gone!"

Out of sight of Eddie . . . yes. Unless, like Arab women, I could hide behind a veil.

"Listen." Mother put her arm around me. "I know you're miserable. I just think you'd be less miserable if you had a change of scene . . . and a change of people."

She didn't say what people, but my father did.

"What's happened to that A&P boy?" he asked. "Is he afraid of poison ivy?"

"No," I said. "I've talked to him on the phone."

He put his newspaper down and looked at me over the top of his glasses. "He called, but he didn't come over. Maybe you didn't encourage him to come over? Maybe you thought he'd run screaming down the street?"

"Oh . . . Daddy . . ."

"Well, he wouldn't. You know, I think you and your poison ivy have been seeing too much of each other, and you exaggerate its importance. But then . . . I'm not a girl, so I don't really know how important these things are. I do remember once your mother got a hairdo she didn't like—and she was right not to like it, it was awful—but I had a terrible time getting her out of the house till it settled down. I guess you like to look your best at all times . . . is that it?"

"Yes," I said . . . for Eddie.

". . . Just a pretty face . . . Well, honey, you're a whole lot more than that. That, too, of course . . . but a whole lot more." He shook his head. "He does seem like a nice fellow, even if he doesn't know enough to smell tomatoes."

Even Marilyn joined this chorus.

"You're almost back to normal, Janet. . . . Are you scared to see him? I mean . . . nervous, like when I haven't seen Jack for a week, and I think, 'What's happened to him in the meantime? What if something's happened?' . . ."

I was, a little . . . maybe a lot. Eddie hadn't called again except once, when I was asleep, and Grandma answered, and forgot to tell me.

"I think you ought to call him," Marilyn said, "and just say, Guess what? I'm back in circulation. Or at least go down to the pizza place tonight so he'll know you're back in circulation."

"Have you seen him there?" I asked.

"I haven't seen him anywhere, except at the A&P. He's *there* every time I go in. He must be working twelve hours a day . . . Oh!" We both lit up like light bulbs. ". . . that's why you haven't heard from him!"

We reasoned this out with impeccable logic. He was working overtime, making up in advance the week he would spend at the youth retreat . . . and another scene took shape in my head, in which we would meet at Lake Clement and Eddie would say, "I was working double shifts. That's why you didn't hear from me," and I would tell him about my poison ivy, and we would enjoy together the fateful coincidence of it all . . . that he couldn't see me at exactly the time when I couldn't be seen.

Marilyn called the night before we were to leave for Lake Clement, to check out what I was going to take. ". . . I packed my radio, so you don't have to bring yours. But I can't find my green bathing suit, and I think I must have left it at your house, so if you find it, will you stick that in? And don't forget your camera. And listen, Janet, I really think you ought to call Eddie, so he'll know for sure that you're going. What if he thinks you aren't going, and so he doesn't go? Think about it."

I did think about it, and concluded that Marilyn had a point. As far as Eddie knew, I'd had some near dread disease, and as far as Eddie knew, I still had it.

And so I called, ready with a speech in which, I hoped, I would sound healthy and happy and confident about myself and him . . . and there was no one home. Later, there was someone home, and talking on the phone, because the line was busy . . . and later still, his little sister answered, giggled, said he wasn't there, giggled again, and hung up before I could say, "Please tell him Janet called, and that I'll see him tomorrow."

Chapter Six 🌿

So when Marilyn and I left for Lake Clement I hadn't seen Eddie in almost three weeks, hadn't heard from him in days, and was as twitchy as Aunt May's cat (from being sat on) at the thought of seeing him again.

We drove to the lake with two other girls and somebody's father, pressed into this service, and since none of us had been there before, we spent most of the trip reading our mimeographed sheets. We were all to sleep in some place called the Hut; there was another dormitory called the Shack; and boys were housed in the Barn. There was also a dining hall and a big open pavilion on the shore of the lake, and two smaller buildings used for study groups.

Anyone crazed for civilization could ignore the number-one rule, "Do not leave the campground," walk ten miles to the nearest town, and turn around and walk the ten miles back. We were later told by an old-timer that there was, every year, one daring group who undertook this pilgrimage.

The Hut turned out to be no hut at all, but a big old farmhouse with a porch halfway around. Inside, it was filled up with cots and cupboards and reminders of past years—above my cot was written JENNY AND PETER, and above Marilyn's, ANNE LYNN SLEPT HERE. Several girls had already put up posters and photographs, and there were stuffed animals everywhere, and a general air of camp camaraderie which surprised and pleased us. I think we expected whitewashed walls and Bible pictures.

My first thought, naturally, was to find Eddie, since he hadn't found me, but Marilyn and I walked all over the campground and up and down the lakefront and past the Barn several times with no success.

"He's probably looking for you," Marilyn said. "We ought to go back to the Hut and just stay there. He might be there now for all you know."

But he wasn't, and there was no note on the downstairs bulletin board to say he had been, and he didn't show up that whole long hot afternoon, and I didn't see him at dinner . . . and I kept wishing that sometime, sometime we had talked about the youth retreat and made some plans; that I had said, "I've never been there before and you have. Where will I meet you?" and he had said, "Meet me at the pavilion" or "I'll come and get you at the Hut." I guess I just thought that he would be there and I would be there, and no matter how many other people were there, or how far-flung the campground, we would spot each other immediately . . . by radar, maybe.

Over the course of the day Marilyn and I joined forces with four other girls from our dormitory—Tinker, Peg, Hattie, and Jewel—who would be, for the rest of the week, our friends, our cohorts, our crowd. We swapped vital statistics (or, at least, whatever we considered vital), addresses, gripes, lipstick, and T-shirts . . . and as soon as it was dark we trailed along with everyone else down to the lakeshore for the bonfire and hymn sing.

"Who is *he*?" Hattie said, jerking her head toward the shadowed perimeter of the crowd. "The one with the blue sweater around his neck."

"Ooooh . . ." said someone else.

The "he" was Eddie . . . lounging at the side of a tall, cool-looking blonde, who was smiling up at him.

"Who?" Loyal Marilyn stared, squinting with great effort, as if he were a personality so dim as to have escaped her notice altogether. "Oh . . . him. He's from our church. His name's Eddie Walsh."

"He's really something," Hattie said, and there was no flip answer for that—he was.

I didn't look in that direction again—looked, in fact, *anywhere* else—but when the hymn sing was over and everybody began to wander off, I did glance over and saw that both Eddie and the girl were gone.

Later that night, as we lay on our lumpy cots, Marilyn said, "I'll bet he doesn't even know you're here. I'll bet he thinks you're still home sick."

"Maybe so," I said.

"And you know what else I think? I think he got stuck with that girl. She sat down next to him, and he was just stuck with her."

We were both quiet then, chewing on these lies. I was pretty sure they *were* lies, but of course I didn't want them to be, so I lay awake, long after everyone else had quit talking and giggling and eating, and managed to turn them into logical facts.

After all, I hadn't seen Eddie in a long time; I hadn't called to say "I'll see you at Lake Clement, I'll be okay by then"; *he* hadn't called to say, "I'll see you at Lake Clement." So naturally when he arrived and didn't see me (so many people, so much ground to cover . . . after all, Marilyn and I didn't see *him* anywhere) he just figured I was still sick. Tomorrow, he would come looking for Marilyn, to find out what the story was.

As for the girl . . . Well, after all, who wouldn't sit down next to Eddie? And, after all, what could he do about it? . . . get up and walk away?

After all . . .

But he didn't come looking for Marilyn the next day, and I soon realized that he wasn't looking for me either.

I saw him after breakfast, walking away from the dining hall, and I started to run after him, to play out the scene I'd made up in my head.

But Eddie had a different script, and, especially, different actors. At the corner of the path he met the tall cool blonde (who probably didn't eat breakfast, or lunch, or dinner, or *food*—just boys, alive), and they walked off, arm in arm, into the happy ending I had plotted for myself.

Marilyn, who was close behind me, saw all this and was neither brisk nor noncommittal, as a casual acquaintance might be.

"Oh, boy!" she said. "What a crud!"

"Which one?"

"Both of them, but especially him."

My feeling was, though . . . especially her. I wasn't ready yet to make Eddie the villain. After all, I was the one who dropped out of sight and left a vacuum which (as we knew from Science I) nature abhors, and hurries up to fill . . . with gas or air or wicked blondes.

"If only I hadn't gotten poison ivy. . . ."

"Well," Marilyn sighed, "it sure didn't help."

This was not especially comforting—"if only" speculations rarely are—but it was something to put a finger on, then and later, as I went over the whole affair, trying to figure out what had happened, what had gone wrong, what I had done, or not done. Here at least was an answer—I had gotten poison ivy. That's what had happened.

That afternoon everybody went down to the lake to swim or lie in the sun, and Eddie was there with the girl, sitting by themselves, away from everyone else but still painfully visible.

"I found out who she is," Tinker said. "Her name's Heather Johnson, and she comes up here every year just to pick up a boyfriend."

Somebody else's, I thought.

"She cuts all the classes and discussions and stays out half the night in the woods. I wonder why they let her keep coming back . . . I mean, to a church camp."

"Maybe they think it'll save her," Marilyn said, thus revealing her true affiliation—the Baptists were hell-bent to save people.

If only I hadn't gotten poison ivy . . . I rolled over on my stomach and pillowed my head on a towel so I wouldn't have to look at them, and even in the hot sun I felt chilled inside, as if I'd swallowed a lot of ice cubes.

"Are you asleep?" Marilyn said after a little while.

"No." I wished I *would* go to sleep, and dream something better than was going on.

"I'm going back to the Hut and see if the mail came. Are you going to stay here, or what?"

"No, I'll go with you."

We took the long way back, around the pavilion and through the woods, on a path all dappled with sunlight through the trees.

"I just can't believe him," Marilyn said, meaning Eddie. "Not even to *say* anything to you."

But I didn't want him to say anything . . . unless it was to say "I thought you weren't coming. I almost didn't come myself. I missed you so much."

We'd shared a whole summer of ordinary things, made extraordinary because we did them together— movies and ball games and dancing at the Colonial . . . walking around town, and climbing the reservoir hill, and sitting in the backyard swing, kissing, to the sound of crickets and the smell of white petunias . . . and sunrise on midsummer swim night.

All that had happened to me, and to him . . . and as long as he didn't come and make me some noble, let's-be-friends-anyway speech, it wouldn't all be over.

My goal, then, was two-fold: to avoid Eddie, and to pretend to myself and everyone else in sight that I was having a wonderful time.

Part of this was pride; part of it, I guess, the hope that Eddie would be impressed by such classy savoir faire; and part of it was simple upbringing, which does crop up more often than you ever think it will— my mother, saying of her lugubrious cousin Edna, "I do get tired of Edna. She might as well wear a sign around her neck, FEEL SORRY FOR ME. But people don't want to feel sorry for you, or to feel guilty because you're miserable and they're not. I want to say to her, 'Edna, get an operation that will lift the corners of your mouth, permanently.' "

I would have welcomed such an operation—by the end of the day my jaws ached from smiling, and I didn't know whether I could keep it up for a week.

Marilyn didn't think I could, or should. "You'll end up biting your fingernails," she said, "from all the tension . . . laughing on the outside, crying on the inside," and then, "I just wish I could help somehow."

"You can," I told her. "Don't tell Tinker or Jewel or any of them, or anybody, about Eddie and me."

"I wouldn't do that anyway. But I can't pretend that *I* don't know."

"And above all," I went on, "don't say anything to him, or to what's-her-name," which was the only way I cared to refer to her.

"Fat chance," Marilyn said. "He avoids me."

Actually, Eddie was avoiding me too. I never saw him except at a distance—but I could see him at almost *any* distance, could pick him out of any group of people; could sense, in the dining hall, when he was coming through the door . . . and, quickly ("Say cheese!"), smile, lean across the table, find someone's eye to meet, as if I were engaged in lively conversation.

What Betty Lou Fultz had told us about the youth retreat turned out to be something of an exaggeration.

There were a few acknowledged camp romances (besides Eddie and what's-her-name)—couples who were always seen hand in hand and couples who were hardly seen at all, and some brief one-day attachments which fizzled out, with no harm done to anyone.

But most of the social life took place on the big wraparound porch at the Hut, where people gathered every evening to talk and drink Cokes and play guitars and sing, and to plot various escapades—midnight raids on the kitchen, ghostly haunting of other dormitories.

I took a determined part in all this. Aside from smiling all the time—"You are such a sunny girl!" one of the chaperones told me, which led Marilyn to observe that perhaps I should plan a career on the stage—I planted myself front and center of all organized and any disorganized activities.

I slunk, with others, into the kitchen very late at night, made off with all the knives and forks and spoons, and hung them from tree branches outside the dining hall—an exercise which took most of the night, but led to a merry and mysterious breakfast, as people tried to find out who did it and, naturally, found out just enough to earn us all points.

The ghostly haunting was more elaborate. There were nine of us, carefully rehearsed in swooping gestures and eerie, high-pitched shrieks, dressed in sheets and gray sheet blankets. This mix of shrouds was a master touch, making us look less like children at

Hallowe'en, and more like a serious company of shades and specters. We held ourselves together with safety pins and string, blackened our eyes with mascara, and smeared zinc oxide on our cheekbones.

"Stay with me," Marilyn said, "because if you don't and I run into you somewhere on the path or in the woods you'll scare the daylights out of me."

We crept down the stairs and into an appropriately dark night with shadows across the moon and wind through the trees—a sound which Hattie proved able to duplicate by whistling through her braces. Our plan was to descend on the Shack, to keen and moan and shriek outside the open windows, and then to swoop through the door, once around the room, and out again, leaving some people scared, some people mystified, and, probably, some people still asleep to be told about it the next day.

But we arrived first at the Barn, and someone said, "Let's go in here."

"I don't think we should go in the boys' dormitory," Jewel said, "I really don't. The chaperones are going to be mad about this anyway and that would really set them off, and I might want to come back next year."

"They aren't going to know who we are," Tinker said. "Would you know who I was, if you didn't already know it was me?"

"Besides," Jewel added, "boys aren't going to just lie there and scream. They'll tackle someone."

In the end some of us stayed out and some of us went in, including me. The whole first floor was one big dormitory room, and in all the clutter and darkness, we would probably have fallen on our faces, except that there were card games going on by flashlight.

We sailed in, between and around cots, with Hattie's whistling braces shrill and piercing in the stillness, and all around us boys woke up, yelled, fell out of bed, grabbed for our trailing sheets and blankets— Jewel was right, boys don't just lie there and scream— and five or six of the card players came in hot pursuit, out the door, and down the path.

We hadn't counted on this and had no contingency plan, but instinctively we split up and took off in nine different directions. I headed for the lake, planning, if necessary, just to dive in and swim away, hoping I wouldn't sink like a stone—

GIRL DROWNS,
ENCUMBERED BY SOGGY BLANKET.

I never got there. Someone caught me, wrapped his arms around me, and yelled, "I've got one!"

Even before he yelled, even though I couldn't see him, I knew it was Eddie. I hadn't expected him to be in the Barn—out in the woods with what's-her-name, I would have thought—and I wished with all my heart that we were back a month in time, at the top of the reservoir hill with his arms around me, the way it used to be.

"It's a bunch of girls from the Hut," someone yelled, and Eddie said, "Is that a fact? . . ."

I broke away then, and ran on down the path.

He could have caught me—I was swaddled in my blanket and couldn't see where I was going, and he could have caught me—but he didn't even try. I looked back once and saw the shape of him still standing in the middle of the path, and then he turned and walked away.

Did he know it was me, I wondered, under the scary makeup and the ghostly garb? Suppose I had said, "It's me, Eddie" . . . what then?

I had never considered this possibility—that *I* would be the one to say something, to make the overture, to clear the air. As I walked back, the long way, to the Hut I thought about what I might say, and what, then, he might say, and how it might turn out, after all, to be a simple case of signals crossed . . . like stories in which the hero waits behind a lamppost on Valley Road North for the heroine, who is waiting behind a lamppost on Valley Road South, for the hero, until they both give up and go away and live out the rest of their lives heartbroken and alone . . . all because neither one dared to say "Where were you?"; to say "What happened?"; to say *something*.

I was the last one back to the Hut. "Where were you?" Marilyn said. "I was just about to come and look. I thought they caught you."

"Who . . . the boys?"

"Or Mrs. Hildebrand. She heard all the racket and

went to see what it was, and then came and made a little speech about tempering good fun with good judgment. Then, you know what else she said? She said, 'I suppose, though, that now we'll have this ghosts and goblins caper every year.'"

"And, listen." Hattie leaned over from her cot. "We're going to walk into town tomorrow. We're going to start early, like daybreak . . . and if you have any food stashed away, bring it along."

That figured. We had, apparently, started a new tradition, so we were the obvious people to carry out an old one.

Even so, we were a grumpy group the next morning when we staggered down the stairs to begin what Tinker called the Long March.

Long . . . I guess. Of course, ten miles is no terrible distance, but it is longer to walk when you are doing it than when someone is telling you about it, as in . . . "It's about ten miles to town" . . . and by midmorning we were like little children on a trip, asking every five minutes, "Are we almost there?"

"We must be almost there," Peg said, rubbing her feet. We'd stopped for the umpteenth time to rest, to shake loose gravel from our shoes, and to wonder (also for the umpteenth time) how this ever got to be a tradition at the church camp.

"Why not just throw somebody in the lake?" Tinker grumbled. "That would be better, and quicker . . . and cooler."

It was steamy hot, and by the time we got to town we were soaking wet, footsore, thirsty, and starved, and we stumbled into the drugstore as if it were an oasis in the middle of the desert.

It was, in a way—the only commercial establishment around as far as we could tell: part drugstore, part grocery store, part gas station, part post office. But there was a Coke machine outside the door, and the proprietor ("I'm Orrie Gamble," he told us) cranked six Cokes out and gave them to us . . . "On the house. Once a year, on the house, for you must be the girls from the church camp."

Here, we thought, was a touch of fame.

"It beats me why some of you do this every year, but anyone who'll tramp ten miles just for the glory of it and then tramp ten miles back deserves a Coke in the middle."

He was not the only game in town, he told us. There was a feed and grain store, farther down, and McCandless's Department Store, and the Grange Hall and two churches. "But your bunch never seems to care to go much beyond me. Not that I blame you," he laughed, "for it's just as far going back. But maybe some farmer'll happen along and give you a ride."

None did, and it seemed not only just as far but infinitely farther, and we straggled back, strung out along the road like the remnants of some exhausted army.

"Penny for your thoughts," Marilyn said, as much, I think, to break the silence as anything else.

"How much farther it's going to be," I said.

Had we been alone, I would probably have told her what I was really thinking, and had been thinking, off and on, all day—that I must find a way, make an opportunity, to talk to Eddie. I could say (very cool and worldly), "We really can't go on avoiding each other as if we were strangers. Let's not be strangers, Eddie"; or maybe (all brisk business) something along the lines of wanting to know where we stood, as if I just might have other fish to fry. Or maybe— and this, of course, was my favorite—I wouldn't have to say anything at all. I would contrive somehow to find him alone, just the two of us, and *he* would say how miserable he had been (appearances to the contrary), that he hadn't known what to say to me, that he didn't think I cared anymore. And I would say . . . And he would say . . .

These were my thoughts as we slogged back, too tired finally to know what we were doing or where we were going. Jewel and I took off our sneakers and couldn't bear to put them on again and went the last three or four miles barefoot, hardly conscious of the stones and gravel we were walking over.

As we turned the last bend in the road, and saw the gates of the camp ahead, Marilyn stopped. "You know what," she said. "I just remembered. Tonight's the square dance. We have to go to a square dance."

"We have to go to *bed*," Hattie said. "I can't go to a square dance! You have to dance with everybody at a square dance!"

And everybody has to dance with you, I thought. That's the way it works. You have to dance with the short fat boys, and the tall skinny boys, and the boys who walk all over your feet . . . and then, to even things up, you get to dance with the boys you've had your eye on all the time.

Sometime, in the course of the square dance, I would find myself with Eddie . . . if my feet didn't fall off first.

Chapter Seven 🌿

I think you're crazy," Tinker said. She was sitting on a cot, with her feet in a pan of hot water. "You'll be crippled for a week."

I thought she was probably right, and more than anything else I wanted to join the crowd and soak *my* feet in a pan of hot water.

Only Marilyn knew why I was so determined to go to the square dance. "I guess I'd probably go too," she said, "if it were me. I couldn't stand to go on the way you are . . . as if you didn't even know him. Do you want me to go with you? I won't dance, but I could sit down somewhere and eat popcorn."

"No, that's okay."

"Do you want to wear my sneakers? My feet are bigger than yours."

So I went to the square dance wearing Marilyn's sneakers, and though no one met me with bouquets and brass bands, there was a modest general cheer on behalf of the girls who had made the traditional walk to town. Somebody made a medal out of crushed aluminum foil and pinned it on me, and somebody else made a trophy out of Styrofoam cups and lettered it with all our names.

And I danced—not very well and especially not very fast, with one nervous partner after another, most of whom said, "Don't you want to sit down? Maybe you better sit down."

No one really knew how to square dance, so there was a lot of confusion, with people getting mixed up and going the wrong way, and finally, in a grand right and left, I saw Eddie coming toward me around the circle.

I'll just take his arm, I thought, and pull him right out of the dance and out of the hall. I'll just say, "I want to talk to you . . ." and no one will even notice or pay any attention.

But suddenly there he was in front of me, hand-to-hand, not looking at me . . . looking past me, looking down at the ground, looking anywhere else. I said, "Eddie, I want . . ." and stopped, because my voice was so shaky and my throat so tight. I knew if I tried to say any more I would cry . . . and I knew, too, that nothing I could say would make any difference; that there was no big misunderstanding; that there wasn't going to be any happy ending.

I saw him end up with Heather, and they linked arms for the grand march, laughing, as if this was just the way they'd planned it.

I left then, and hobbled down to the lake and stood there with my feet in the cool wet sand, listening to the crickets and the frogs, watching the path of moonlight on the water . . . numb with longing and regret.

When I got back Mrs. Hildebrand fixed me a pan of hot water. "Now you put your feet in there," she said, "and don't you take them out. I never heard of such a thing . . . to walk twenty miles and then go to a square dance!" She also gave me her bedroom slippers—big ugly boats of brown felt, with teddy bears stitched on the uppers.

"I ordered them out of a catalog, for my little nephew," she said. "I told them size four, but this was what they sent. Can you beat that?"

I knew she was just trying to help, but I wanted her to go away and leave me alone, and when she did I put my head in the pillow and cried . . . quietly, so I wouldn't wake Marilyn or Tinker or Jewel or any of them. Sometimes you want people to know you're crying, and sometimes you don't.

I woke up early the next morning, but Marilyn was already awake. "What happened?" she whispered. "What did he say?"

"Nothing. Neither did I. It really wasn't such a good idea."

Tinker sat up in bed. "What wasn't a good idea?"

"To go to the square dance," I said.

"I'll say not . . . are you okay, though?"

"Oh, sure . . . just my feet still hurt."

"What a crud he is!" Marilyn said under her breath, so only I would hear, and know she was with me.

I wore Mrs. Hildebrand's slippers for the last two days of the retreat. I didn't *have* to, my feet were okay . . . but they turned out to be a mark of distinction, like wearing a cast for everyone to sign. You'd rather not to have to wear the cast, but you do the best you can with it. I was the girl in the teddy bear slippers, the girl who walked twenty miles and then went dancing. I wore my aluminum medal too, and my pasted-on grin, and on the last day when everyone ran around taking pictures of the Hut and the Shack and the lake, about thirty people took pictures of me and my feet.

We drove back late Sunday afternoon and were deposited at the church to be picked up by parents— Marilyn's father, in our case.

"Would you go again?" Marilyn asked, as we rode home.

"I don't think so. Besides, I'll have a job . . . you too. We'll be working."

"That's right." Marilyn's father looked at us in the rearview mirror. "Next summer you'll be working girls. That'll mean some changes. You may not care for all of them."

"I don't know . . ." I said. "I think I will." I liked the sound of it, and the idea of it—*I have a job; I don't have time to think about Eddie; I have to go to work.*

"We could take time off," Marilyn said. "That's what lots of people do—the Lambert twins, and Brenda Coe, and Eddie . . ." She stopped. "I'm sorry. I was just thinking of people who worked and . . ."

"Listen," I said. "Don't be sorry. You were right, he's a crud. I couldn't care less."

We were both quiet then, uncomfortable and a little stiff because you shouldn't have to put up any front for your best friend. We had always told each other everything, and now I'd shut Marilyn out with a big brave lie. Lay that to Eddie, too, I thought—the spoiler.

It was dark by the time I got home, and the porch light was on for me—something of a concession because it brought all the bugs to cluster on the screen. I could hear the radio going someplace, and the murmur of voices someplace else, and kitchen sounds— water running, and dishes being dried and put away.

I took no comfort from all these familiar things, and I suddenly wondered why Aunt May chose to come home when her heart was broken.

I wanted to go straight to the Greyhound bus depot and take a bus to somewhere far away and start over— a mysterious figure with no past. "She went off to the Methodist youth retreat," people would say, "and that was the last anyone knew."

"Is that you, honey?" Mother called. "Come in quick so the bugs don't get in."

No bugs got in but the cat got out—a scratching streak of gray past my legs—and right behind him, Aunt May, with everybody else right behind her.

"Oh, that cat!" Mother said. "He just waits there at the door. May! May!"

"She's gone off without a stitch of clothes on but her nightgown," Grandma said. "She'll get arrested running around the streets in her nightgown."

"Here's a raincoat." My father brushed past me out the door, with a coat over his arm while Grandma yelled, "She's gone up the street," and Mother called out the door, "May, wait a minute!"

Then she turned and threw up her hands. "Oh, I don't know."

I suppose I had pictured a homecoming scene . . . What was it like? they would ask? What did you do? Tell us all about it. . . . Expecting to hear happy things, for happiness, after all, was supposed to be my natural condition. This is the happiest time of your life, people were always saying.

Now, instead, I seemed to be mostly in the way of the cat chase, and by the time everybody got back (except the cat) and asked for an account of my adventures, I felt, nose-out-of-joint, that I was pretty much back-page news.

"What in the world have you got on your feet?" Mother wanted to know . . . and I chose to be airy and offhand. We had walked to town, that was all . . . twenty miles. And then I had gone dancing and hadn't been able to get my shoes on since, that was all.

Reactions were immediate and quite satisfactory. Why had I done such a foolish thing? Where were the people in charge? Did I know that I could have ruined my feet? For the second time my mother threw up her hands and said, "Oh, I don't know" . . . and I felt that I had matched the cat, in terms of exasperation.

I took my suitcase upstairs and unpacked—clean clothes and dirty clothes, Marilyn's white shorts, my aluminum medal, crushed by now into a little ball, and when everything else was out, a sifting of sand in all the corners and cracks—the last remnant of the Methodist youth retreat where, according to Betty Lou Fultz, ". . . everyone pairs up with someone. It's terrific!"

As I climbed into bed I heard the weather report on Aunt May's radio: ". . . mid seventies tomorrow. Outlook for the week, bright and sunny. Get ready for a perfect summer day!"

I hated him, and his cheerful voice, and his cheerful weather report . . . and all perfect summer days.

Chapter Eight 🌿

I kept my eyes shut while everyone else came up to bed and, passing me, pulled the sheet up to my chin, or patted my head, or kissed me. That was my mother, who never failed to kiss me good night. ". . . As long as you're within reach," she always said, "however old you get to be."

I sometimes fussed about this, but I really liked it, and planned to do the same thing with my own children, along with never yelling at them or requiring them to eat carrots. They were vague in my mind, these children, although when we were younger Marilyn and I had said exactly what they would be—a boy and a girl for each of us, mine to be named Peter and Penny, hers to be named Beth and Brent. It was hard to believe, now, that we had ever been that young, or that confident about arranging our own destinies. I hadn't been very good, lately, about arranging my own destiny.

Unable to sleep, I propped my pillow up in the window frame and tortured myself by staring at the backyard swing where I had sat so many times with Eddie, his blue-sweatered arm around my shoulders, his face close to mine. It was like biting on a sore tooth to remember these details: it hurt, but I couldn't stop doing it.

Because I was the only one awake I was the only one who heard the cat, mewing piteously at the back door, and I went down to let him in.

He was a battered object—scratched, clawed, bleeding, with great clumps of fur missing here and there. I didn't know what to do, and while I stood there wondering whether iodine would kill or cure a cat, or simply send him crawling up the walls, Aunt May appeared in the door. She swooped down on the casualty and wrapped him up in the first thing that fell to her hand—my mother's white Sunday tablecloth.

"Oh, the poor thing!" she crooned, cradling cat and cloth in her arms.

Was this going to be Pansy all over again, I wondered? And if so, what would that do to Aunt May . . . not in a general way, but right now at two o'clock in the morning, in the kitchen, with everyone asleep except me?

. . . A man she loved but couldn't marry; a dog

she loved, run over by another man she'd married but didn't love, or loved and changed her mind about, I didn't know which; and now a cat she'd adopted off the street, fed, loved, and made us all put up with . . . loved and lost, loved and lost. It seemed like a terrible toll.

"Is the cat going to die?" I asked.

"No." She examined his ravaged face. "None of the cuts are that deep, thank God. Besides, cats heal themselves . . . it's a good trick." She lit a cigarette and squinted at me through the smoke. "What kind of a time did you have at Lake Clement? I used to go to Lake Clement when I was a girl. I remember once we drove up in George Lawson's new Packard and George let me drive it and I ran over a chicken. George paid the farmer for his chicken, but I felt terrible anyway." She went on stroking the cat, whispering in its ear, "Poor kitty. Poor kitty."

"Who was George Lawson?"

"Just a boy I knew."

Had she loved him, I wondered? Had she, maybe, married him and nobody happened to tell me about that one?

"He was Cramer's cousin . . . Cramer Gentry. That was how I came to meet Cramer, because we all went around together in those days. And we had good times." She stared past me out the window, the streetlight shining on her face.

"We went on hayrides a lot, all of us piled into some farmer's wagon. There were dances too, on Saturday nights in the American Legion hall . . . and parties. I even remember the dresses I wore. There was an apricot crepe de chine . . ." She put her hand to her hair, as if to smooth it to whatever style was suited to the crepe de chine. "I had a coat with a gray fur collar that hooked right under my chin, soft as a kitten." She didn't say any more then for a few minutes, and the only sounds were the kitchen clock and the low hum of the refrigerator . . . and the cat, purring softly now, as Aunt May rubbed behind his ears.

"But then everybody began to split apart or couple off," she went on finally. "People moved away. One of the boys ended up in Congress, one of them ended up in the state penitentiary. Mary Haney went to China as a missionary—last thing anybody expected Mary Haney to do. Another girl married a dirt farmer from Adams County . . . fourteen children the last I heard. Funny how things work out. You think if only this or that had happened . . ."

Aunt May didn't go to bed at all that night. My mother found her the next morning. ". . . sound asleep, with her head on the kitchen table, and that cat wrapped up in my tablecloth and a saucer of milk gone sour on the floor beside my laundry basket. What in the world happened?"

"The cat got in a fight or something," I said. "He was all cut up and bloody. We thought he was dying."

"Well . . . poor thing." Mother took a minute to

examine the cat. "But wouldn't you know that with drawers full of kitchen towels, the thing May would pick to wrap him up in would be my best tablecloth?"

But that morning my sympathies were with Aunt May—what little sympathy I could spare from myself. "Mother, he was bleeding all over the place. You don't stop to think about tablecloths when your cat is dying."

"My." Mother looked at me. "That's a new tune for you. Though it might be a good thing if you've had a change of heart about the cat—you can take over the care of him when May leaves."

"Is she leaving?"

"Well, she'll be leaving sometime, and sometime pretty soon, I expect. They certainly won't keep her job for her forever."

"You mean she's going back there? To Detroit?"

"Why, yes. Why not? Where else would she go?"

"Someplace different, and start all over."

Mother shook her head. "Very few people start all over. That's why you hear about the ones who do. Most people just take up where they are and go on from there . . . and nobody knows that better than May."

Mother was right. Over the next day or two Aunt May began to pack her suitcases. She went to the Beauty Nook and had her hair done and she bought herself a new fall outfit right out of the window of the French Mode dress shop . . . and when she came downstairs, ready to leave, you would have said, had you been there, that this was no heartbroken woman.

"I don't know why it is," Mother said, eyeing the dress, "that I can never find a thing to suit me at that dress shop. May, if you want to get the five-o'clock train you'd better call a taxi now. You know they take a while," and then, as Aunt May produced a boxlike contraption, "What's that?"

"It's a cat carrier."

"You surely don't expect to take that cat with you? Especially when he was sick and bleeding all over my tablecloth?"

"Oh, he'll be fine in a few days. Cats heal themselves in a hurry." She grinned at Mother. "Be a lot easier for you if people did the same, wouldn't it, Jane?"

"Now, May . . ." Mother hugged her and then went to work picking cat hairs off the French Mode dress. "Don't you talk like that, or think like that. After all, what's a family for?"

I felt confused and vaguely betrayed, as though Aunt May had let me down in some way, and while everyone bustled around—calling the taxi, jamming the cat into his box, arguing about whether Aunt May should take half an apple pie and a jar of bean soup all the way to Detroit on the train—I stayed out of the way.

I kept remembering Aunt May the night she stood in the hall with tears in her eyes, clutching the telephone, saying "I just want to talk to him." I hadn't done that yet, but I had dialed Eddie's number and then hung up. I was pretty sure I would do it again too, just to hear him say, "Hello . . . hello. Who is this?" It was contact we wanted, Aunt May and I. We didn't want it to be over.

And yet, here was Aunt May, all dressed up and hair-done, acting for all the world as if she had swept her heartbreak under the rug.

She left the same way she had arrived, with a lot of sound and fury—yelling to the cabdriver to wait a minute, calling for her coat, looking for her hat, retrieving cigarette packages from the top of the piano, the china cabinet, the buffet; big, noisy smacks all around; and then she was gone . . . bag, baggage, cat, apple pie, and bean soup.

Mother stood up at the front door, shaking her head. "May's like a cat herself," she said. "Wades into trouble, retires to lick her wounds, smooths her fur, and bounces back. When the Lord puts together people like May, he must put lots of rubber into the mix."

Later she and Grandma went to the kitchen to work over the tablecloth with more bleach and bluing and elbow grease. My father went out back to water the lawn, and I put on my teddy bear slippers and took a walk around the block . . . and then another block, and all around the neighborhood, thinking all the while how remarkable it was that life was going on all over the place just as though I'd never known an Eddie Walsh, let alone loved and lost him.

And lost him—hard knowledge, this—for no romantic reason (incurable illness, untimely death, feuding families); no grand and gothic reason upon which I might build a life of reclusive habits and mysterious sorrow. I had lost Eddie—as I would no doubt lose, and gain, much over the years—simply because things change.

I went to bed in my own room that night but I couldn't sleep—too many echoes everywhere of Aunt May's testy presence.

So finally, like Aunt May herself, I went roaming around in the night—down the dark stairs and through the silent house, in which I had spent all the years of my life so far, and would spend more to come, until time and circumstances moved me someplace else . . . where I would probably keep oilcloth on the kitchen table and family pictures on the mantel, plant white petunias outside the back door, and hang a swing from some convenient tree; carrying pieces of the past to lean on, much as Aunt May, when in need of support, came home.

I went upstairs to the rollaway cot and propped my pillow in the window frame. This had become more my place than any other in the house, even though it was temporary . . . or maybe *because* it was temporary. I had just begun to realize how temporary all our places are.

About midnight it began to rain—big drops splashing down through the leaves and against the house, and then, before long, a gentle steady patter.

I was very tired and my head kept dropping forward against the window screen, but I didn't want to go to sleep. How would it be, I wondered, if all of time could stop right now, for me, at this uncomplicated moment: fresh summer rain, green summer smells, pale streetlight shining on the wet sidewalk . . . and so I tried to stay awake, as if nothing would change, as long as I was looking at it.

The clouds had blown away and there was a bright path of moonlight across the yard, like a ribbon rolling out smooth and straight, disappearing in the darkness beyond Grandma's rose bed.

People's lives are like that, I thought. They start out straight and shining and unruffled—Marilyn saying, "Isn't everything perfect!" when, for a little bit of time, it was—but no one could see the whole length of the ribbon. I had tripped over a big wrinkle—I thought of Aunt May, racketing off to Detroit in her French Mode dress with her strange encumbrances, black and blue from tripping over wrinkles—but our ribbons rolled on just the same . . . to what place? to what person?

One thing was sure—you couldn't just sit down and quit, for fear of stumbling over other wrinkles.

I stared out beyond the rosebushes. There were brambles out there, and garter snakes . . . but there were white violets too, and wild huckleberries, and the occasional surprise of smoky, magical Indian pipes . . . out there in the darkness.